of
Criminals
by
Evelyn James

A Clara Fitzgerald Mystery
Book 4

Red Raven Publications

Cover images copyright
(Anagoria; Doroneko; Emillie & Lloyd; Libens Libenter; Richard Ash; Texnik)

© Evelyn James 2014

First published 2014
Red Raven Publications

The right of Evelyn James to be identified as the Author of this work has been asserted in accordance with the Copyrights, Designs and Patents Act 1988.

All rights reserved. No part of this book may be reprinted or reproduced or utilised in any form or by any electronic, mechanical or other means, now known or hereafter invented, including photocopying and recording, or in any information storage or retrieval system without the permission in writing from the author

Other Books in
The Clara Fitzgerald Series

Memories of the Dead
Flight of Fancy
Murder in Mink

Chapter One

Clara Fitzgerald maintained a polite façade of interest as the rather decrepit woman sitting opposite her gazed into a scratched crystal ball. The name over the tent had read Gypsy Rose, Queen of the Fortune Tellers. It had been as much impatience as curiosity that had driven Clara into the tent. She hated waiting for people, it made her all twitchy, and the tent had offered a five-minute distraction. Besides, Gypsy Rose had looked rather forlorn all alone in her tent – the fortune telling business had seen better days.

"I see you meeting…" Gypsy Rose had a Romany accent and wore a lot of black lace, particularly over her head. She appeared to be aged around eighty, "…a tall, dark stranger. Very dark, indeed. Oh, but…"

Gypsy Rose stopped waving her arms mystically over the glass ball and propped a pair of gold pince-nez on the bridge of her nose. She squinted hard into the crystal ball. When she looked back at Clara the Romany accent had disintegrated into a broad Yorkshire brogue.

"Dearie, I only tell it as the ball says it, so don't get in a dither, but I see you meeting a tall, dark stranger and… urm… he'll be dead."

Gypsy Rose bit her lip waiting for Clara to scream or

shriek outrage at her for such a ghastly fortune. Clara, Brighton's first female private detective, merely laughed.

"You would be surprised how often that is the case." She rose, deposited a sixpence in the bewildered fortune-teller's hand, and left the tent reflecting that Gypsy Rose was undervaluing herself.

Outside it was a beautiful August day, the sun was high in the sky and the air rang with the laughter of children. Clara was standing in the middle of a fairground on Brighton Green, with music and excitement all around her, which made it seem all the more remarkable that Clara could feel so morose. Many would have considered her setting if not idyllic, certainly happy. Unfortunately Clara could not help that August made her feel sorrowful; the summer was drawing to its close, the flowers had bloomed and mostly gone past their best, the roses in the garden were overblown and smelt sickly sweet, the bees buzzed frantically around them as though sensing their time was running out. The trees looked dry and tired, the grass was yellow and dead. Everyone complained of the heat and the sulphuric smell coming out of the sewers.

Before long the leaves would go golden and orange, summer would be gone for another year and it would be the long trek back into winter; frosty mornings, icy afternoons, chilly evenings. It all added up to a strange fug that lingered over Clara and made her feel quite depressed when really she should be enjoying these last hazy days of sunshine.

Of course it didn't help that six years ago the Great War began on just such a sunny August day. It only seemed to compound, in Clara's mind, that August marked the end of things.

"Fresh Scotch toffee?"

Clara was shaken from her doldrums by the arrival of her brother and a paper bag of creamy, tan-coloured toffee.

"Stop looking so miserable." He instructed as he thrust the bag at her.

Clara gave a small sigh as she dug her hand into the bag, deciding that her attempts to develop a slim-line boyish figure (as was all the rage) had once again been thwarted. Tommy grinned up at her from his wheelchair.

"We just saw the ugly lady, as I predicted she is one fine pig dressed in a frock. Gloucester Old Spot, I should say."

"I was rather relieved that was all she was." Annie, the Fitzgeralds' maid and firm friend, said rather primly. She had come up behind Tommy bearing three stone bottles of lemonade, "After all, if every ugly lady had to run away to the circus to earn a living, Brighton would quickly be emptied."

"Annie!" Clara said in mock horror, accepting the lemonade proffered towards her.

"I exclude us, of course." Annie amended her earlier comment, "Anyway, are we going to take a look at the performing monkeys? I heard tell they sing and dance."

"Don't believe all you hear." Clara smiled as they started to head into the heart of the fair, "I was just told by Gypsy Rose that I would meet a tall, dark stranger who would be very dead."

"She must have heard of your reputation." Tommy asserted with a shrug.

"Perhaps." Clara answered.

Brighton had not seen a funfair since those glorious summer days of 1913. War had dampened the spirits and made travelling shows difficult. Workmen and performers were called up into the army and the logistics of carting dozens of wagons and attractions across the country became impossible. Not to mention all the horses who were also conscripted for service at the Front. The English fairground had almost ceased to exist during those four long, dark years. Then peace returned and the showmen pulled their rides and engines out of the yards and fields where they had been stored. They cleaned them down, tarted them up, found new horses or invested in a steam engine, and the show was back on the road. After so long without the bright, bawdy carnival attractions of the funfair, the arrival of carousels, freak-shows, coconut shies and the myriad of other novelties that went with the fairground had struck delight into all but the hardest heart. What had once seemed tawdry and old-fashioned in the glamour days of Edwardian Brighton, now seemed fresh, vivid and alive. Just like the spirit of good old Britain. A lick of paint and both were as good as new.

The fairground that had come to Brighton had certainly made the most of the opportunity. There were around 100 stalls and attractions scattered along the seafront. Clara had spotted two carousels, the stars of the show with their leering horses and spinning mirrors. There was a huge helter skelter, a swing chair, and a dizzying whirler. Dotted among them were tents containing everything from discreet films of an adult nature to snakes and lizards, not to mention the food vendors and the wide array of smaller games, such as the bowling alley and rifle range. Clara wasn't entirely clear whether this was one large fair or several small ones that had banded together. But whatever the case, they had certainly put on a fine show.

"Isn't that Colonel Brandt?" Annie motioned with her hand to a gentleman leaving a large white tent.

"I do believe it is, he looks a little pale." Clara watched as Colonel Brandt mopped his brow with a large handkerchief.

He had just emerged from beneath a sign that read Exotic Birds, Delightful Creatures from all Four Corners of the Globe. Either side of the words were painted two scantily clad women, cunningly avoiding public scandal by the strategic placement of large palm leaves. A sign near the entrance read Adults Only and a surly looking fellow barred entrance to anyone who had yet to pay, which pretty much told Clara all she needed to know about the attractions inside.

"Colonel Brandt."

The colonel looked up and his face went crimson. He

daubed furiously at his brow with the hanky and looked a little faint. Clara hurried forward and took his arm.

"Are you all right colonel?"

"Just had a bit of a shock, that's all. I misunderstood the context of that sign," Colonel Brandt was about to wave behind him, then remembered he was speaking to a lady and did not want to add to his embarrassment, "I never saw anything like that in India."

"Never mind colonel, would you care for a cup of tea?"

"Yes, I would. I was expecting parakeets you know."

They found their way to a stall selling hot drinks and ordered four cups of tea. Then they arranged themselves on a verge of grass between two stalls and all began sharing their experiences of the morning. Tommy had seen his first crocodile, though admittedly it had been a small one and rather disappointing. Annie had ventured into a food tent and learned a new way of making dumplings. Brandt had explored most of the animal tents, up until his fateful arrival at the Exotic Birds. Only Clara had little to share, having spent most of her time wandering rather aimlessly, her mind on other things.

"I haven't seen a proper vulture in years." Colonel Brandt was explaining, waving his teacup around rather perilously, "Ugly critters, but smart as a dog. I swear if I could tame one I would be quite inclined to keep it as a pet."

"But would you not have to keep feeding it sheep carcasses and such." Tommy observed, ignoring Annie's outraged look at the mention of such an unpleasant topic as deceased farm animals.

"I imagine I could work around that. Not sure my housekeeper would approve." Brandt slurped his tea, "Well Miss Fitzgerald, tell me what case are you working on at the moment?"

"I am case-less." Clara answered, "Since we returned from our cousin's abortive wedding, I have had nothing in particular to work on. Unless you count that little matter of the elderly gentleman who had lost his glass eye. I found it in a rather unsavoury place."

"I say! A picture house?" Gasped the colonel.

Clara laughed.

"No, in his maid's bedroom. Bundled in some rather personal laundry. I imagine it was accidental."

"Old men do a lot of things accidentally." The colonel gave her a theatrical wink and Clara started to wonder if he had really wandered into that colourful tent under the mistaken belief it would be full of birds of the feathered variety.

"If we are all done with our tea, might I suggest we try the House of Curios?" Tommy nodded to a distant marquee with a large sign outside proclaiming it contained many ancient wonders, "I am always game for a laugh."

The four of them headed for the pale green tent which had a steady footfall of curious onlookers entering its canvas doorway. There was no attendant for this particular display and several Bright Young Things had taken advantage of the large displays and dim recesses of the tent for a spot of canoodling. As was the way of things, everyone was pretending not to notice them. Tommy, however, was not everyone.

"Why look, that is Mrs Barker's lad! Hellooo young Freddy Barker! Who is your friend? Why the delightful Miss Brown from the paper bag factory. How unexpected to see you two together when dear Mrs Barker was just saying how she was hoping you would get in with Penny Draper who lived two houses down."

"Gosh, isn't that Deirdre from the library? What ho, Deirdre. I don't suppose you know if my book on typography came in? Oh, I see you are with a fellow, don't let me bother you. Did you realise you had lost a button?"

"Mr Parkinson, what a surprise to see you here Sir. How is the school these days? Isn't that Miss Prim the girls' games mistress standing beside you? She looks a little faint."

Having thus pierced the veil of polite disinterest,

Tommy paved the way for everyone in the tent to now pay close attention to the named persons and their respective partners. Several embarrassed excuses followed of such things as "I was looking for my shoe," "This lady came over a little queer and I brought her into the shade," "We were only discussing cataloguing systems." Having cleared the tent of lovebirds Tommy shook his head and tutted.

"The youth of today."

Clara clipped him lightly around the ear, grinning at his mischief.

"You'll have traumatised them, especially poor Mr Parkinson. He'll never be able to set foot in a tent again."

"He should know better." Tommy answered, "That Miss Prim has more fellows than she does pupils."

Clara chuckled to herself and wandered over to one of the displays in the tent. It proved to be a two-headed calf said to have been born in 1805. It stared at her mournfully from four glass eyes. A faded card noted that superstitious locals thought it's birth a sign of the impending apocalypse because it was born in a violent thunder storm and lived only an hour. The biographer of the unfortunate calf had clearly thought it rather important to note at the end of this grim tale that it was a Hereford from the herd of one Mr P. Oakes.

Clara moved on to a glass cabinet containing alleged pieces of meteorite, one had a nail stuck to it, which the card beside it stated proved it was magnetised. Clara squinted her eyes and spotted a yellowing blob of glue. A further case along proved more interesting. This one was around seven feet tall and contained the lower half of a wooden sarcophagus. Inside the sarcophagus a wizened mummy gaped at them from its wide open jaw. Remains of bandages hung off the shoulders and arms, while a blue scarab dangled from a chain around the mummy's neck. Various glittering golden items ordained the mummy's wrists and fingers, including a rather large ring with a sapphire blue stone. Clara was confident these items were no more than costume jewellery; showmen were charlatans, not fools. She paused to read the printed sign taped to the mummy's case;

"Before you stands the noble pharaoh Hepkaptut, last ruler of the ninth dynasty. His tomb was discovered in 1907 untouched by robbers and with countless priceless relics inside (now safely housed at the British Museum). Hepkaptut was an unfortunate pharaoh who died at the hands of one of his many wives, probably poisoned. He died without an heir and left the Egyptian kingdom in chaos. The scarab you see about his neck was placed there to protect his body in death, clearly a powerful totem as his tomb was unspoiled. He wears gold armbands to denote his royal heritage. Hieroglyphs in his tomb tell us that the ring Hepkaptut wears was a gift from his sister and wife, Neratutu."

"And if you believe that you'll believe anything." Tommy said.

Clara glanced down at him.

"It does look very realistic, as a body I mean. I don't imagine it is a real pharaoh."

"Probably paper-mache stuffed with sawdust." Tommy tapped the glass case, "Nice ring though, looks as though there is an S engraved into the stone."

"All these dead things are giving me the creeps." Annie, just behind them, gave a theatrical shudder, "Could we go look at the monkeys now?"

"From one charade to the next, all right Annie let's go see your singing monkeys." Tommy agreed.

They headed out of the tent and aimed in the rough direction Annie thought the monkey display was in. Clara found her melancholy temporarily lifted by her curiosity about the supposed mummy. Imagine if there really had been a Hepkaptut murdered by one of his wives, she thought, and imagine if his body had been preserved all the way through time to now. He would be the oldest murder victim to still exist. Now, Clara mused, that would be an interesting case to investigate.

Chapter Two

Two days later Clara was in her office working through her accounts when her bell rang. Clara's detective agency was situated above a haberdashery shop, a small set of two rooms up a narrow stairway that served its purpose of keeping her business separate from her private life at home. Unannounced visitors were unusual, however. In general people wrote to her first, outlining their problem before arranging an appointment. Since she had nothing scheduled in her diary, this had to be one of those rare cases of a client just appearing on her doorstep.

Curious, Clara headed downstairs to open the door. She had to admit she was a tad disappointed to see the person standing there was local photographer and friend to the Fitzgeralds, Oliver Bankes. She had been hoping for a new case.

"Hello Oliver."

"Clara, so glad you are in. Can I talk with you?"

Oliver sounded breathless and worried. He had a large brown envelope clutched in his hand.

"Of course, do you want to come upstairs?"

They headed to the office and Clara offered to put a kettle on to boil, but Oliver declined. She motioned for him to sit in an armchair just by the open window, where a breath of fresh air was helping to cool the muggy room.

Clara turned around her desk chair and sat facing him.

"So, what's up?"

"Have you been to the fair?" Oliver pointed his finger in the direction of the sea-front.

"I have. I went with Tommy and Annie."

"Did you go in the House of Curios?"

Clara was worried by Oliver's urgent tone. She was beginning to wonder if someone had taken dangerous offence over Tommy's remarks. Had he upset someone?

"I did yes." Clara said hesitatingly, "Tommy was only japing with the people in there."

Oliver looked blank for a moment, then carried on.

"Did you see the mummy?"

"King Hepkaptut? Yes, what of him? Don't tell me someone has been idiotic enough to break into his case. That jewellery was clearly all fake."

"No, no, the mummy is perfectly safe, it's just…" Oliver suddenly gave a hearty sigh and slumped back in his chair, "When I try and explain all this it stops making sense, even to me. I half wonder if I have gone a little mad."

"Try me." Clara said, her disappointment long abated, "I'm good at things that don't make sense, remember?"

"Well, I am convinced, or at least partly convinced, that I know who King Hepkaptut is, or rather was. And if I am right, then I guess we are looking at a case of murder."

"Are you saying that mummy is real?"

"I'm saying no, it's not a real mummy, and yes, it might be a real corpse." Oliver shook his head, "I told you it didn't make sense."

"No, it makes a sort of sense. The body is real and it somehow ended up masquerading as an Egyptian pharaoh, or so you believe. In that case, who do you think it is?"

"Ah!" Oliver brandished the envelope, "Meet Dog-face Harry, otherwise known to his mother as Mervin Grimes."

Oliver pulled a black and white portrait photograph from the envelope. It showed an unpleasant looking man in his mid-twenties; he was heavy-jawed with ears the size of saucers and a mean stare that glowered at the photographer. He wore a dandy-boy's suit from before the war, and he had a tall bowler clutched in one hand, while he rested the other hand on a table.

"About fifteen years ago Mervin Grimes called into my father's photography shop and asked for a studio portrait. I never knew a more unpleasant man. He scowled the whole time and did nothing but bully and snap at my father. He was a thug, clear as day. Father didn't dare say anything in case of trouble. So he took the photo. I was just taking an interest in photography then. I used to move all the props about for father and help position the sitter. I remember this fellow clear as day, especially that ring on his finger."

Oliver pointed to the photograph where Mervin Grimes was resting his hand on the table. Clara reached over to her desk and picked up a magnifying glass. She held it over the image and peered at the hand. There was certainly a large ring on his finger.

"He was the sort of man you never forget. Well yesterday, when I walked into the House of Curios, I got the shock of my life when I looked into a case and there was Mervin Grimes staring back at me."

"King Hepkaptut? How could you possibly recognise that wizened corpse as anybody?"

"By the ears first off and something about his face, the way he was scowling. All right, so I know that isn't conclusive. But that's where I come to the ring. I swear the ring that man is wearing in the photograph is the same as the one on the mummy's hand in the fairground."

Clara peered through the magnifying glass again.

"It's difficult to be certain."

"That's pretty much what the police said."

Clara stiffened.

"You went to the police first?"

Oliver opened his mouth, then closed it as he recognised his error.

"I thought they would seize the body. Sorry Clara."

Clara let it go. She put aside the scowling image of Mervin Grimes, then turned back to Oliver.

"So, let's start with this logically. Are we certain Mervin Grimes is dead?"

"Mervin Grimes vanished not long after that portrait shot was taken. The police were looking for him and there was a notice in the paper for anyone with information to contact them. As far as I am aware he was never found."

"In that case, assuming Mervin really is dead, how did he end up mummified? Or, for that matter, in a fairground?"

"I don't know." Oliver admitted.

"Funny place to put a corpse, where everyone can see it."

"But as you say, who would recognise him like that?"

"You." Clara said simply, "Of course that is assuming that whoever runs the House of Curios had any knowledge that their latest exhibit had once been Mervin Grimes. If it is Mervin Grimes."

"Clara, you see that we have to investigate this, don't you?"

Clara found herself looking at the photograph again.

"It is certainly curious, but basing this on a ring alone is hardly conclusively. Mervin might have lost or sold the ring, it might not even be the same one."

"True, but if it is?"

"Then it is certainly worthy of investigation. Let's start with the basics; our only clue is that queer ring on king Hepkaptut's finger, which doesn't look very Egyptian to me. If we could identify that ring as conclusively once belonging to Mervin Grimes, it would be a start. I don't suppose you have any other photos of Grimes that show the ring in a better light?"

"I would have to ask father." Oliver admitted, "He might remember it also."

"Let's do that first and then we will need to take another look at this mummy."

"Thanks Clara, for believing me." Oliver smiled.

Clara gave a shrug.

"Someone had to." Then she winked at him.

Oliver escorted Clara to his father's house down Clifton Hill. The modest terrace sat in the middle of the row, set back from the road behind a scrubby patch of grass one might loosely consider a front garden. Oliver opened a short black gate and stood back to let Clara through.

"Clara, before you meet him, you should know that my father is rather an odd soul."

Clara paused and looked back at Oliver.

"In what way?"

"Just eccentric. He has funny ways. I'm afraid he may have been exposed to too many of the developing chemicals in the shop."

"Will he be able to help us then?"

"Oh yes, he has all his marbles. Well, all the ones that count."

Oliver hastened to the front door and rang the bell.

"I live in the flat over the shop these days." He explained almost apologetically, as if feeling the need to defend his decision, "Father gets a bit lonely, I think."

The bell echoed in a hallway beyond the door and there was the sound of footsteps. The door opened and an old man with grey hair and a sergeant-major moustache greeted them. He had an antimacassar perched on his head. Clara tried not to stare.

"Father! What have you got on your head!" Oliver couldn't believe his eyes, mortified at the appearance of his parent.

"What? Is my toupee on the wrong way?" Bankes senior reached up and patted his head.

"That isn't your toupee!" Oliver groaned, his horror growing.

Mr Bankes snatched the antimacassar off his head,

revealing a bald pate, and scowled at it.

"Oh bother." He smiled an apology to his son, "I must have muddled them up."

Clara had been trying to contain a stifled giggle, finding the whole situation both preposterous and amusing. She now presented her hand to Mr Bankes.

"Clara Fitzgerald." She introduced herself.

"Father, we have come to discuss some of your old photographs." Oliver regained the conversation, "This is my friend Clara, she is a private detective."

"Really?" Mr Bankes stared at Clara, "But she looks like a woman?"

Oliver actually blushed as his father blundered from one faux pas to the next. Clara merely took it with amusement, she had heard far worse in her short time as a detective.

"Could we come in?" Oliver said in a strained voice.

"Naturally. Would you like a cup of tea?" Mr Bankes moved back from the door and motioned to his front room, "I was cataloguing some old images, don't mind the mess."

As Mr Bankes went off to make tea, Oliver led Clara into the front room and gave another groan. Every chair, table and flat surface (including some of the floor) was covered with photographs. Sitting among them were pieces of card with writing on such as "Parks, Brighton", "Seaside, Punch and Judy, 1907-1910" and "Unknown, misc. scenes". Most of the images however seemed to have been scattered with little consideration for the category they might best conform to.

"I'm sorry about this Clara. He is always inventing new filing systems and dragging all his pictures out to re-sort them. He gets very particular about them." Oliver illustrated his point by picking up two cards. The first read "pigeons, grey", the second "pigeons, white (doves?)", "Most people would be just content with labelling them under pigeon, or even just birds."

Oliver scooped photographs off a chair in irritation,

depositing them in a heap on a card table already overflowing with pictures. He offered the now empty chair to Clara. She sat down on something soft and furry.

"I think this is the toupee." She proffered the grey hairpiece to Oliver.

He just shook his head and perched it on top of a porcelain dog sitting on the mantelpiece.

"Ah, do you mind no milk?" Mr Bankes appeared in the doorway looking sheepish, "I thought I had some, but it appears to have gone off. My 'help' doesn't call in until lunchtime, you see."

"Let's not worry about tea." Clara decided to act as a peacemaker, seeing the look of mild fury developing on Oliver's face, "Perhaps we should just get to the point of why we are here?"

"Oh yes, why are you here?" Mr Bankes perched himself on the arm of a chair, "Oliver normally only comes on a Sunday. It isn't Sunday, is it?"

"No, it's Wednesday." Oliver said through gritted teeth.

"I thought as much." Mr Bankes nodded, "Sorry, I lose track of time being at home all day."

"Look father, we came about a photograph you took years ago." Oliver produced the envelope he had been carrying around, "Do you remember this fellow?"

Mr Bankes took the image of Mervin Grimes and peered at it for a bit. He reached over to a side-table and dug among some photos for a pair of round glasses. He propped them on his nose and studied the picture again.

"24 May 1905. Mr M. Grimes, paid three shillings but never collected his pictures. That is the country-house prop set, including fake Sheridan table. Very popular with those looking for a formal backdrop. It's very classical."

"You actually remember the date?" Clara said, incredulous.

"I remember everything about my pictures." Mr Bankes didn't look up from the image, "Mr Grimes came in the day before wanting his photo taken because he had just come into some money. He had bought a new bowler hat in celebration. I arranged for him to return the next day and I took the picture. He was very precise with what he wanted, which was why I was surprised he never came back for the photos."

"Mervin Grimes vanished." Oliver said.

"When?"

"Just after the picture was taken, I'm not sure of the exact date. Do you remember anything else about him?" Oliver pressed.

"Such as?" Mr Bankes studied the picture a little longer, "I remember I didn't like him. Thought he was a street thug dressed in better clothes than he deserved. But he was a customer, so you put up with these things."

Oliver was visibly disappointed his father had not mentioned the ring.

"Mr Bankes, did you happen to take other pictures than the one you are holding of Mr Grimes?" Clara asked, as she carefully retrieved a crumpled photograph she had accidentally sat on.

Mr Bankes scratched his chin.

"For three shillings I wasn't going to take a lot of time over him." He said, "I took a seated picture. I call it the casual pose. The sitter leans back in an armchair with one hand lightly resting on their knee. The other arm is positioned with the elbow on the chair arm and the sitter's chin perched on the hand. It gives a relaxed charm to the final photo. Mr Grimes was not very accommodating with that."

"Mr Bankes, think carefully, which hand does the sitter rest on their knee?"

Mr Bankes gave Clara an odd look.

"Depends on the person."

"And do you have this second picture of Mr Grimes?"

"Look now you two, what is going on?" Mr Bankes, who at first had seemed rather vague, now revealed he had not lost all his marbles, "Has Mr Grimes been found?"

"That is the thing, I'm not sure." Oliver looked bleak, "But maybe, yes."

"And you are trying to identify him? Why haven't you told the police?"

"They aren't interested at the moment." Oliver shrugged, "They think I am chasing shadows."

"But that other photo might help?"

"Maybe. Hopefully."

Mr Bankes whistled through his teeth.

"It will be filed under portraits, 1905, May, Male, Single Sitter, G." Mr Bankes slapped down the photo in his hand, "And there wasn't a copy in the office filing cabinet? Right. And it was never collected. Give me a moment."

Mr Bankes disappeared from the room.

"Your father seems nice." Clara said to Oliver, doing her hardest to smooth out the photo she had sat on now Mr Bankes couldn't see her.

"He's a tad eccentric and embarrassing." Oliver ran a hand through his dark hair, still feeling mortified over the antimacassar.

Clara smiled at him.

"At least he isn't boring."

"Oh, he's not that!"

"Why did he give up photography?"

"He hasn't." Oliver said, "Just the business. No, he still takes pics in his spare time. I don't know what of because he has never shown me."

"Perhaps because you have never asked?"

"Don't go making a fellow feel guilty here, Clara." Oliver protested, "I try my hardest, but I have a shop to run."

"I'm interfering again, aren't I?" Clara sighed.

"Only a little, and it's one of the things that makes you a grand detective." Oliver grinned at her, "I'm rather excited to be working on a case with you."

"It's not a case yet."

"But it will be, I hope."

There was a noise on the stairs and Mr Bankes briefly sailed past the doorway.

"Not upstairs, going to try the footlocker in the conservatory." He called as he vanished.

"See?" Oliver said to Clara in exasperation.

"He is being very helpful." She defended Mr Bankes.

They waited patiently a little longer. Oliver pointing out a couple of pictures on the walls he had taken, including one of Loch Ness in Scotland.

"I was after the monster."

Clara rolled her eyes.

"Really Oliver, and you say your father is eccentric?"

Oliver laughed.

It was at that moment Mr Bankes reappeared holding a photograph.

"I had filed it under T for Time waster. I must start keeping better track of my system." He proffered the photo to Oliver, "Any good?"

Oliver looked at the picture and then turned it over to Clara. She took a good look at the figure and in particular his right hand which was resting on his knee.

"Can you do that clever thing where you take a small detail in a picture and make it bigger?" She asked.

"A blow-up of his hand? Yes, of course, it probably won't be very clear, though." Oliver took back the picture, "It will take a little while."

"Then I suggest we arrange to meet at seven o'clock. Mr Bankes, how do you fancy a trip to the funfair?"

Mr Bankes looked at Clara bemused.

"Tonight?"

"Precisely. How does that sound with you Oliver?"

"I'll have the picture ready." Oliver agreed.

"Then I will see you tonight, seven o'clock at your shop. Bring a magnifying glass and both pictures of Mervin Grimes."

"This is very curious." Mr Bankes muttered, scratching at his chin again.

"It will get even more curious before the night is out if

Oliver is right." Clara said sinisterly.

Chapter Three

Fairgrounds come alive at night, with their bright bulbs and gaudy colours. The shadows of darkness mask their defects and for a few short hours they burst with glamour and glitz, before daylight dispels the illusion and shows up all the cracks. But the fairground at night, along with the innocent fun-lover, also attracts the dubious element, those who favour darkness over the stark glare of daylight. Under normal circumstances Clara would have much preferred to stay away from the fair at night, even if seven o'clock in summertime was not exactly pitch black. Still, there was definitely an air of trouble pervading over the tents and amusements, not helped by the presence of several police constables.

Brighton was a popular holiday spot for London gangsters, assisted by the lure of seasonal racing. City prostitutes were also notorious for taking a trip to the seaside on the tail of wealthy holiday-makers. A short train ride from London was all it took to escape the smog and smoke of London and breathe fresh sea air. Not to mention it was a handy cooling-off spot for anyone who found themselves in trouble in the capital. Clara loved her hometown, but she had to admit it had a dark side that scared her.

Oliver met her promptly at seven outside his shop. He

was sporting a striped summer jacket and a straw boater. She couldn't resist tapping her finger on the latter.

"Expecting a boat ride?"

"You don't appreciate a man trying to look smart for you." Oliver said with mock hurt in his tone.

Clara laughed.

"So you are trying to look smart for me now, Oliver Bankes?"

Oliver winked at her.

"Don't expect my father to be on time, by the way. I don't think he knows the meaning of punctuality."

Oliver was right; it was nearly half an hour before Mr Bankes wandered along the road. In the meantime Oliver had popped over to a Lyons teashop and persuaded a Nippy to let him abscond with two cups filled with tea. He and Clara had drunk them perched on the sill of his shop window.

"Sorry I'm late folks, damn watch has stopped again." Mr Bankes doffed his bowler hat to them, apparently missing Oliver's disgruntled look.

They walked together to the entrance of the fairground. It was thruppence to enter, a token price to keep the tramps and vagrants out, once inside the showmen knew exactly how to squeeze every last penny out of their visitors.

Having been to the show once already, Clara found the dazzle less exciting than before. The novelty had most definitely worn off. Oliver on the other hand looked eager to try everything and already had his eye on the rifle range, which was offering jars of cocoa as prizes for a perfect score. He couldn't remember the last time he had gone to bed on a good mug of cocoa. Mr Bankes was meanwhile staring at the big wheel which could be seen spinning over the tops of the tents. He whistled through his teeth.

"If only I was younger."

"Before we all get swept away, should we head for the House of Curios?" Clara suggested, her own instincts telling her to keep an eye on her handbag in the large crowds now circulating the fair. Every moment she stood there, the fair seemed to lose more and more of its sparkle. Not helped by some decidedly dubious fellows who were loitering around the best rides for no obvious reason. She had a nasty feeling something was going to happen tonight.

Oliver distracted himself long enough from the lure of cocoa to lead the way through the fairground to the tent marked House of Curios. It might have been quiet earlier in the day, but tonight the tent was buzzing with people wandering in and out, gasping and giggling at the objects on display. A wooden cigar store Indian now stood just outside the door, a sign hung around his neck informing everyone – "See the Mermaid of Syria! Goggle at the Two-Headed Calf! Marvel at the headless chicken that lived for a week!"

"Are we ready to meet Mervin Grimes?" Clara asked her two companions.

Oliver gave a grimace. Mr Bankes showed no sign he had heard anything, but followed them as they entered the tent. It was packed with people and difficult to move through. The mournful calf was still staring out of its case with its baleful eyes and attracting a suitably shocked audience. Clara had to do a bit of polite barging to squeeze through to the glass case containing King Hepkaptut, or at least the place where the glass case had stood. For the good pharaoh was mysteriously gone and in his place stood a large stuff bear that a sign declared was the very creature shot by Davey Crockett as it mauled him.

"Where is Hepkaptut?" Oliver said in astonishment.

Clara crouched down and plucked something out of the grass. It was a small fragment of glass.

"Oliver, who else did you tell about your suspicions?"

"No one except the police."

"Hmm." Clara tossed the piece of glass back to the ground, "I think we better find the man in charge of this place. Something very curious is going on. I'm starting to think you are onto something Oliver."

Oliver grinned.

"Really?"

"Yes. Now where on earth do we find the fairground manager?"

He wasn't as hard to find as might be imagined. After asking for directions off a few stall holders they were shown to a large showmen's caravan in the centre of the fair. It was smartly painted and bore the name on the side 'Bowmen's Touring Carnival'. A large van that normally towed the caravan was pulled up discreetly to one side. Clara hopped up the two steps to the door and rapped loudly. She could only hope Mr Bowmen was in and not abroad keeping an eye on his showground.

After a moment there were sounds of movement and the door opened outwards forcing Clara back a step.

"Yeah?" The man peering out of the caravan was in his forties, dressed in pale trousers and a white shirt. He wore no waistcoat or jacket, but had a cloth napkin tucked into his collar. He glowered into the night looking belligerent, while the hand he rested on the doorframe still held a fork. They had interrupted him in the middle of dinner.

"Clara Fitzgerald." Clara offered him a card, which he didn't look at, "We would like to speak to you about the matter of King Hepkaptut."

If anything Bowmen's expression grew more malignant.

"He ain't for sale." He went to slam the door shut, but Clara saw it coming and stood in front of it, so he would have to drag her into the caravan if he wanted to close the door.

"I'm not interested in buying. I am interesting in discussing exactly who Hepkaptut is, or rather was. I think you really would want to talk to us, if you understood." The showmen didn't look impressed so she quickly pressed on, "There is a secret concerning that mummy, and if the signs in the House of Curios are anything to go by we are not the only ones to realise that. Before anything worse happens, I suggest we talk."

"Are you threatening me?" Demanded Bowmen.

"Absolutely not. I am trying to help."

"I don't need any help."

"Perhaps not yet, but we really must talk. Else, I will have to take the matter up with the police and allow them to investigate a possible murder."

"Murder?" That had caught his attention, "What are you talking about?"

"Do you really want to discuss this on your doorstep? We are talking about a very serious crime."

Bowmen hesitated, then he reluctantly took a step back and motioned for Clara to enter. Oliver quickly jumped up behind her, but when Mr Bankes went to follow, Bowmen blocked the way.

"Not enough room!" He snapped and slammed the door in his face.

Inside the caravan the main portion was set up like an ordinary parlour. Two snug armchairs sat either side of a modest fireplace, over which hung a huge mirror. The walls were ornamented with posters of acts past and present, along with a small bookcase that boasted the complete set of Dickens. At the front of the caravan a plank swung down from the wall to act as a table and on it sat Mr Bowmen's dinner of liver and potatoes. Bowmen sat himself down at the table and dug back into his meal, shovelling a large piece of liver into his mouth before he turned back to Clara and Oliver.

"Well? What's this about Hepkaptut?"

Clara glanced at Oliver. There was, of course, always the possibility that Bowmen knew the true identity of the mummy and had in fact been instrumental in his death. But Clara thought that unlikely, most murderers were not insane enough to put their victims on display, even when they did run a fairground.

"Perhaps you better show him the photograph Oliver?"

Oliver produced the brown envelope once more and removed the picture of Mervin Grimes. He offered it to Bowmen who glared at it without putting down his fork.

"Who's this?"

"The man we believe became Hepkaptut." Clara explained, "Unless, of course, you have proof that the mummy in your House of Curios is thousands of years old."

Bowmen caught the hint of sarcasm in Clara's tone.

"I just buy the things, if someone tells me it's an Egyptian mummy what came out of a tomb who am I to argue?" He said defensively, "Anyway, this fellow don't look like Hepkaptut."

"I admit the resemblance is not exactly plain to see." Clara nudged Oliver, "The other photo Oliver, please."

Oliver produced a second picture, an enlargement from the seated portrait Mr Bankes had found. It showed Mervin Grimes' hand.

"Please note the curious ring on his finger Mr Bowmen, I think you may have seen it before?" Clara held the photo before Bowmen's nose.

He glowered at the image, then some of his anger turned into fear. His eyes went back to Clara.

"So the mummy is wearing Mervin Grimes' ring, doesn't mean it is Mervin Grimes."

"That is true, but I think it warrants further investigation. Besides, we are forgetting that someone attempted to steal your mummy this afternoon, didn't they?"

"I figured it was kids fooling around." Bowmen grumbled, "They smashed the glass. Fortunately one of the workmen was passing and heard the commotion. He shouted and ran into the tent, but whoever it was had run out the other exit. They hadn't had a chance to take anything."

"I personally suspect that someone else knows this is

Mervin Grimes. Someone who isn't keen on his body being on display." Clara turned the picture of the ring to face her, "Mervin Grimes hung around with some very unpleasant people. Not the sort you want loitering around your fairground. Where have you put Hepkaptut?"

"He's locked up in the bearded lady's caravan." Bowmen stabbed at a potato and swirled it round in greasy gravy, before shoving it in his mouth, "No one will be getting it from there in a hurry."

"With your permission I would like to take Hepkaptut to someone who can properly confirm if he really is Mervin Grimes. I should add that, if that proves to be the case, the police will want to take him and ultimately his body will be returned to his family, I imagine."

"And I lose my mummy." Bowmen snarled.

"In the scheme of things it is a small sacrifice. Besides, would you rather I tell the police you have a modern murder victim on display?" Clara fixed him with her most determined stare.

Bowmen gritted his teeth, but he knew he was in no position to argue. Besides, who wants a suspected murder victim's corpse on their hands?

"If it isn't Mervin Grimes, I get my mummy back." He stated, a slither of liver on his fork.

"I imagine so." Clara replied.

"Give me your card again."

Clara handed over one of her cards which read; "Clara Fitzgerald, Private investigator" and gave her office address. Bowmen turned it over in his hands.

"So I know how to find you." He said, placing the card on the table.

"I'll keep you informed of what happens." Clara promised.

"Well if you want the mummy you best find Jane Porter, she's our bearded lady and the only one with a key to her caravan. Tell her Derek said it was all right for you to take Hepkaptut, not that she is likely to argue, she doesn't much want that thing in her caravan." Bowmen wafted his fork at them, "And if it does turn out to be Mervin Grimes I want nothing to do with it. I bought Hepkaptut a year ago in good faith. I didn't kill anyone."

"Thank you Mr Bowmen, I will bear that in mind."

Bowmen huffed.

"Is that it?"

"Yes." Clara knew when she had outstayed her welcome, "Shall we let ourselves out?"

"Go right ahead, you didn't seem worried about letting yourselves in."

Clara turned to Oliver and they left the caravan, feeling Bowmen's venomous glare follow them all the way. Back in the fairground they discovered Mr Bankes had vanished.

"Do you want to go find him?" Clara asked.

"He can look after himself." Oliver shrugged, "Besides, I'm not leaving you unescorted."

Clara rolled her eyes. She hardly considered herself in any danger, at least, not yet.

"I suppose we must track down the bearded lady, I suggest we head over to the rather offensively titled freak show." She said.

"You know, with most bearded ladies it's all fake." Oliver said as they headed in the direction of a number of large tents, "A bit of glue and suitable hair is all you need. Though I dare say some are real."

"Poor creatures." Clara replied, "To live your life always mocked or derided by others because of an unfortunate quirk in the fabric of one's body. I feel extremely sorry for the likes of Jane Porter."

"At least she has the fair." Oliver mused.

"That is hardly a just compensation."

They aimed for Gypsy Rose's stand since Clara recalled seeing a sign for the freak show near her stall. The fortune teller's tent was doing a mediocre trade, considering Gypsy Rose's talents Clara found that rather surprising. She gave the old lady a little wave, feeling sympathetic to her plight. They headed around the back of some more tents and came upon a sign that indicated the freak show was nearby. A motley crowd of gawkers had gathered around a raised platform, no wider than six foot, and were listening to a man in a tatty evening suit telling them about the vagaries of Mother Nature and the cruel fates she could inflict on the unfortunate.

"Wait for it, he'll be telling us next the mothers of these sad souls were traumatised while pregnant and that caused the deformities." Oliver said in Clara's ear.

"You've seen a show like this before?"

"I always came and watched the freak show when I was a boy, didn't realise then that these poor people were truly deformed in some way. I thought it was all faked. Modelling clay and wax, that sort of thing. It never occurred to me these people look like this all the time."

"It is very sad." Clara said just as a man with no arms appeared on the stage. The announcer explained to the crowd that the unlucky gentleman had been born this way, but they seemed unimpressed. Considering at least one man in the audience was also missing a limb from his time in the war, parading an armless man on stage seemed rather poor taste. The announcer in the tattered evening suit sallied on valiantly, informing his crowd that "Armless Arnold" (as the man was unfortunately known) was a talented artist, using only his feet. Arnold attempted to display his bipedal dexterity by drawing on a large canvas, but the audience had already lost interest and were moving away.

In a desperate bid to lure them back the announcer quickly revealed "Yan-Ging and Gin-Yang" Siamese twins from Singapore. The appearance of the two petite ladies in a single red dress briefly stopped the exodus, especially when they began performing acrobatics for the mildly stunned crowd.

"I've seen enough." Clara hissed to Oliver, "Let's go around the back and see if we can't find the bearded lady."

"Do you suppose those two are really joined at the hip?" Oliver couldn't take his eyes off the performing twins as he followed Clara around the back of the tent.

"Does it matter?" Clara asked.

"I just wondered if it was easier to perform those moves they did with four feet rather than just two."

Clara couldn't decide if he was joking or serious. She shook her head and motioned to a flap in the tent. They both ducked and went inside.

If they had expected to find a bustling backstage area, like the sort found at the theatre, they were quickly disabused of the idea. Aside from a couple of upturned wooden crates, the only furniture in the tent, if such it could be called, were straw bales upon which a motley assortment of the deformed and socially unacceptable sat miserably awaiting their turn. Armless Arnold was propped on one bale, twisting a pencil between his toes. Behind him the Siamese Twins were just coming off stage to be replaced by two dwarves dressed in jester outfits. Further acts dotted about the cramped space included a girl who was attempting to stitch her legs into a fake mermaid tail, a man with an extra finger on each hand who was dressed as a magician and an old woman with horns growing out of her head. Clara found the whole sight very depressing.

"Excuse me," She turned to Armless Arnold who gave her a sad smile, "I am looking for Jane Porter, is she here?"

"Behind that screen." Arnold pointed with one foot to the far side of the tent.

"The public aren't supposed to be back here." The girl in the mermaid tail primly told Clara.

"I'm not the public." Clara answered back, "Nice tail."

The girl snorted.

"What is this about?" The man with six fingers looked up from a deck of cards he was shuffling.

"Nothing that need concern anyone here. It is unrelated to the show." Clara started moving through the straw bales.

"Maybe Jane's been at it again." One of the Siamese

twins, it might have been Yan-Ging, said in a stage whisper, "You know, with one of her fancy men. She get herself in trouble."

"The mind boggles." Oliver said as he hurried behind Clara.

"Clearly some men are taken by beards." Clara grinned as she stopped before the screen. She gave a polite cough and announced herself, "Miss Porter? Might I have a word with you, it will be very brief. My name is Clara Fitzgerald."

There was a rustling behind the screen.

"I have to go on stage in a bit." A strained feminine voice called back.

"It will only take a moment. I just need to borrow your caravan key."

There was a pause and then the screen was pulled back a fraction.

"Whatever for?" Half a face was peeking around the screen, it was round and distinctly hairless.

"I have permission from Mr Bowmen to take Hepkaptut's mummy into my safe keeping."

"Oh thank goodness!" The face disappeared and then a shaking hand stretched around the screen with a key, "I hate that wretched thing. I went to have a nap this afternoon and when I awoke the pharaoh had fallen over onto my bed. The shock of seeing this desiccated dead face peering at me caused me to…"

The screen moved back and Jane Porter, professional bearded lady, stared at them with teary eyes as she presented her hairless chin.

"The fright made my beard fall out." Jane gave a sob and half collapsed onto a straw bale, "I'm ruined!"

"Oh dear." Clara said softly, crouching in front of the formerly bearded lady, "That is such a pity. It will grow back, I imagine."

"Do you really think so?"

"Yes, I'm sure it was just the surprise. Give it a few days and you'll see some stubble coming back."

Jane dabbed at her eyes with a handkerchief.

"Th...thank you. It's not much of a life, but show business is all I have got."

"Naturally. Don't take it so hard though. Perhaps take a short holiday until things start to improve."

Jane gave a little nod.

"And you are removing Hepkaptut now?"

"Hopefully." Clara answered, the thought crossing her mind that moving a mummy through a crowded fairground might not be the easiest of endeavours.

"I'll show you to my caravan, I can't go on like this anyway."

Jane Porter escorted them out of the tent and a short distance away to a portion of the fair that was marginally quieter and was clearly a private area for performers' caravans. She motioned to one that had been painted red with gold filigree work all over the sides.

"That's Arnold's work." Jane pointed out, "He has a lot of talent."

"He does indeed." Clara noted the crisp lines of the paintwork. Who would have thought someone could paint like that with their feet.

"Well, there's Hepkaptut." Jane had unlocked the door and was pointing inside.

King Hepkaptut was leaning propped against a built-in cupboard, staring at them with closed, blackened eyes. He looked rather despondent, if that was possible for a corpse.

"Exactly how are we going to carry Hepkaptut home without drawing untoward attention to ourselves?" Oliver asked the question that had been bothering Clara.

"Oh Bowmen had him rolled up in a carpet." Jane interrupted. She kicked a rug with her foot, "You can use that if you like."

Clara and Oliver exchanged a look that echoed the surreal nature of the situation they were now in.

"Oh well." Clara shrugged, "I'll grab his head if you take his feet."

It was not easy negotiating the mummy onto the rug in the cramped space of the caravan. Jane was no help, fearful that if she got too close to the mummy she would end up beardless for life.

"I swear he is cursed." She said through the doorway as the reluctant pharaoh finally made his way onto the carpet, "Everyone who goes near him has bad luck. It is some Ancient Egyptian magic."

"Well Mervin Grimes certainly had some bad luck." Clara muttered to herself.

"I'll be most relieved when he is out of the fair. Why did you say you were taking him anyway?"

"For safety, because of the attempted thefts." Oliver quickly answered, "We're from Brighton Museum, you see."

"Ah, that makes complete sense." Jane nodded, "I wondered why anyone could want an old mummy. Is he worth a lot?"

"Not really." Oliver hastily added, "But not everyone realises that. They think if something is old enough it must be worth a fortune and, as he is of historical value, we felt it wise to take him under our care."

"I see, I see." Jane agreed enthusiastically.

Clara gave Oliver a questioning look from where she was trying to wrap the mummy in carpet. Oliver returned the look with a wink and leant forward to help. Five minutes later they were leaving the caravan with a rather fat roll of carpet.

"Thank you Jane." Clara said.

"My pleasure." Jane could hardly contain her relief to have her caravan back to herself.

Oliver took the lead as they headed out of the fair, keeping the top of the carpet as high up as was possible to avoid people looking in the roll and seeing Hepkaptut.

"Brighton museum?" Clara asked as soon as they were out of earshot of Jane.

"I had to say something." Oliver shrugged, "Why else would I want a mummy?"

"Why indeed." Clara answered, beginning to feel that her life had taken another of those curious twists that it seemed rather fond of, "I say, we never did find your father."

"He'll turn up." Oliver said happily, "He always does."

They exited the fairground and followed the sea wall along the front, Hepkaptut bouncing in his carpet roll.

"I must admit this is the weirdest thing I have ever done." Oliver mused, "Rather puts an end to my plan for finishing the evening with a hot coffee at Lyons."

"Once you have dropped this at my house you will still have time to go. They open until nine."

"I think you missed my point."

Clara reconsidered his statement and it dawned on her what he had actually been trying to say.

"Oh." She was silent a moment, "You know, Annie makes a jolly good coffee. It would be the least I could do, after tonight's events, but to offer you a drink before you leave for home."

"It would be damn impolite of me to refuse."

"It would indeed."

Oliver grinned.

"I accept your invitation Clara Fitzgerald."

"Jolly good." Clara smiled, "Because you didn't have the option of refusing."

Chapter Four

There were two things Tommy really detested in this life; one was waiting, the other was having to visit the doctor. Naturally quite often these two hated things came together at once, producing an effect of such tension and frustration in Tommy that he would swear to himself he would never be forced to do either again unless he was dying. Of course, Tommy had at one time thought he was dying. It was during that long, cold night in No Man's Land, when he stared at the stars and tried not to cry out in pain. He still remembered the chilling sensation of the Flanders mud seeping into his clothing and the terror that he might be sucked beneath it and drowned – he had seen that happen before to men and horses.

When they found him he was almost delirious with pain. A bullet had shattered into his pelvis, crippling him and leaving him in agony. They came for him in a brief lull in the shelling. The stretcher men ducking as they nipped over the mud, hoping to avoid an enemy bullet. It was one of those all too infrequent moments when both sides called an unofficial ceasefire so they could collect their wounded. You just had to hope you were rescued before some uptight colonel spotted the truce and ordered the bullets to come hurtling again.

Tommy had been lucky. Not that he had felt lucky at the time or, for that matter, for many months afterwards. He had never walked since, though the doctors in the military hospital were convinced he should be able to. Nothing medically wrong with the legs, they would continually state. Well, in that case, why can't I move them? Tommy would retort. And they would just shrug and silently imply it was something to do with his thinking. As if Tommy hadn't tried to move his legs! Wouldn't he love to get up and walk if he could?

After three years of immobility Tommy had surrendered the small amount of hope he had left that he would ever walk again. What was the point of holding on to such illusions? He had to get on with his life, even if it was not what he had expected it would be. Naturally he was bitter about it, hard not to be, but one made the best of things, didn't one?

Which made him wonder all the more why he had allowed Clara to convince him to do that most hated of things – visit a doctor. Here he was in the front parlour-cum-waiting room of a man called Dr Cutt (which name alone failed to inspire confidence) awaiting yet another verdict of "nothing we can do." Annie had wheeled him there and gone to do the shopping, he assumed this was so she could avoid being persuaded to take him home before seeing the doctor. There was something terribly humiliating about knowing your actions and choices were dictated by the presence of other people. Tommy found his mood rapidly going from merely frustrated to morose. A young man should not find himself immobile, he told himself, better to have died than live as an invalid.

He was about ready to let himself tumble into despair when a head appeared around the parlour door.

"Mr Fitzgerald?" A man with a broad round face and small glasses smiled at him. He had to be eighty at least, "Very pleased to see you could make the appointment."

Dr Cutt held out his hand and Tommy shook it.

"Your sister informed me of your problem, I hope I

may be of service." Dr Cutt took the handles of the wheelchair Tommy sat in and pushed him through the doorway and down a hall. They turned right into a back room which served as the doctor's surgery, "Now then, what appears to be the matter?"

Dr Cutt took a chair by a desk as Tommy stared at him incredulously. The doctor raised an eyebrow indicating he was awaiting an answer.

"My legs, obviously." Tommy almost spluttered. His sister had clearly lost her marbles sending him here.

"Yes, but what is the matter with them?" Persisted the doctor.

"They don't work."

"Yes, but why?"

Tommy found himself without an answer, or at least one that was polite. What sort of a fool was this man? He had been shot and left for dead, for goodness sake, of course his legs didn't work after that! But the doctor was still waiting for him to answer the question, smiling patiently. Finally Tommy gave in.

"I don't know."

"And nor do your doctors, apparently." Dr Cutt tapped a finger on a grey cardboard folder at his elbow, "I requested your notes from the military hospital, I know one of the doctors there. According to these papers there is no reason for you to be crippled. There was a lot of tissue damage for sure, but the nerves were intact. You can feel pain in your feet and toes yes?"

"Well, yes."

"There you are then. Nerves are the messenger boys of our body. If they are disconnected or damaged the messages don't get through. But you, my lad, you have all your message routes intact. So the question remains, why can't you walk?"

"I thought maybe something wasn't connected properly?" Tommy said weakly.

"Your legs are made up of bones, muscles and nerves, oh and blood vessels of course, but for our purposes bones, muscles and nerves will do." Dr Cutt stood and opened a cupboard, on the inside of which was a chart of a human body showing its inside workings, "I keep this hidden as it disturbs some of my old ladies." Dr Cutt smiled, "Here is a drawing of the legs with the muscles and nerves. So, the bones are your foundations, the scaffold. Break one of those and it is painful, it may even heal wrong and leave you with a twisted leg, but once it is mended you will be able to walk on it, right?"

"I suppose."

"Of course, I even know of patients who have carried on walking on a broken leg without realising. Now, as for the muscles," Dr Cutt pointed at the muscles coloured in pink on the drawing, "They can be damaged, cut, withered, but they restore themselves. They might be weakened, but even then they can be strengthened. Unless they are removed completely or reduced to pulp they will heal and become functional once more. Do I make myself clear?"

Tommy nodded.

"So to the nerves. Nerves are the vital bit and quite frankly we still need to know a lot more about them. What we do know is that if you break the path from the nerves to the brain a person may think about moving their limbs, but that message will never reach its destination. In short, broken nerves are the cause of many cases of paralysis. Now, here is the interesting part. Nerves also tell us about pain and other sensations. A good indicator that nerves are damaged is when a person cannot feel pain in their extremities."

"But I do feel pain."

"Precisely."

"So my nerves aren't broken?"

"Not physically, no." Dr Cutt closed the cupboard door, "Now we come to the delicate part. When all the body appears to be functioning as it should physically then we naturally have to assume there a psychological aspect to the problem."

"It's in my head, you mean?" Tommy started to feel angry, "Look I have tried to move my legs, tried and tried. You think I want to be stuck in this chair? I lay in that hospital bed for hours trying to get my legs to work. I'm not deliberately stopping my legs from working!"

"You misunderstand me." Dr Cutt held up his hands in a placating manner, "Or rather I explained myself badly. I don't think you are deliberately crippling yourself Mr Fitzgerald, at least not consciously."

"Then what do you mean?" Tommy was close to letting his frustration get the better of him.

"The mind is very complicated. Have you heard of Dr Freud?"

"Yes." Tommy admitted.

"He proposed the idea of a conscious and unconscious mind. It is a fascinating idea we are only just beginning to grasp. Say there are two parts of the mind, the part that we use all the time, that we are using right now, that is completely in our control and then the other part, the part that operates outside our control."

Tommy wasn't much into psychology and his expression said as much.

"For instance, sometimes your body reacts to things that you were not consciously aware of. Say, while asleep. Your body will react to an outside stimulus even though you are not awake to tell it to do so. Something is controlling it. We are starting to think of this something as the 'sub-conscious' and we are learning, through scientific experiments, that it is exceedingly powerful."

"I don't see how this has any bearing on my legs."

"It could be that there is a barrier in your sub-conscious, a mental fence that is preventing you from moving your legs. It is interfering with the messages."

"Why? Why would my own body not want to walk again?"

"This is not about the body." Dr Cutt smiled softly, "The body is a mere machine, it has no wants or desires of its own. It is the mind that wants, that thinks, that feels.

And the mind is a fragile thing which can so easily be damaged. Tell me, do you have nightmares?"

Tommy shuffled in his chair.

"Sometimes."

"The same ones?"

"Usually."

"Have you ever heard of shell-shock?"

Tommy gave him an odd look, then he mumbled.

"There were some mutterings in the hospital."

"Shell-shock is a form of mental trauma no different to a broken arm or stab wound, except it is in the mind and very difficult to treat with traditional methods. Mr Fitzgerald, some elements of the medical community, myself included, believe that as many as 8 out of 10 men who served in the trenches has been affected in some manner by shell-shock. It comes out in different forms. Some men seem to go crazy, others are described as losing their nerve and many more have far more subtle symptoms, such as nightmares. It is nothing to be ashamed of."

Tommy didn't agree with him, but he said nothing.

"Still I see you don't believe me. That is all right, but I want you to start considering the possibility that it is shell-shock that is preventing you from walking. It is damage to your sub-conscious mind that has not healed. You are neither mad nor weak, any more than a man with a broken arm is mad or weak." Dr Cutt realised his patient didn't believe him, "Let's try something, anyway. Your sister said that sometimes your legs move when you are only semi-conscious. With your permission I will give you a mild sedative and we shall see if we can encourage your sub-conscious to let go its paralysing hold on your legs."

Tommy hesitated. He didn't like the things Dr Cutt had said. The idea that his mind was damaged in some way troubled him, implied that he was somehow defective. He had hated how the doctors had implied the same thing at the hospital. Admittedly they had done so in a dismissive manner, whereas Dr Cutt seemed genuinely sympathetic. Dr Cutt gave him another kind smile.

"I realise that we live in a world that doesn't approve of people having damaged minds. We are going to have to learn to get over that. So many men came back damaged in ways no ordinary surgeon can fix."

Tommy swallowed hard, there was a painful tightness in his throat.

"The military doctors gave me the impression they thought I was faking my inability to walk." He said quietly, "I've never even told my sister that. I'm ashamed that I am like this. Ashamed that I was never able to go back and carry on fighting. If this really is in my head, then those doctors were right. I let my friends down, I let my country down, because my mind wouldn't let me walk. If you're right then… I'm a coward."

"Thomas Fitzgerald," Dr Cutt leaned forward, his voice was gentle but firm, "No man is a coward because he is injured and unable to fight. Did I not say that your mind was injured in a way you could not help? Just because you cannot see an injury does not mean it is not there. If a man has his eardrum pierced it is not visible on the outside, but his injury nonetheless makes him deaf. Do not be swayed by fools who think the mind is a mere tool to be used as we see fit. It is far more wonderful than that and far more delicate. Something happened to your mind. Had it been pierced by a bullet the military doctors would have understood, it is only because they can't see the bullet that got you that they shake their heads. Don't listen to them."

Tommy stared at his hands for a long time. There was a wedge of emotion in his chest that prevented him from speaking. The worst of it was the horrid anger he felt towards himself, the anger that not only had he been injured in the first place, but that he had not been able to recover.

"My grandson was in the war."

Dr Cutt's voice broke into Tommy's bubble of self-loathing. He risked looking up.

"He was an army doctor. He saw so much horror, it overwhelmed him." Dr Cutt picked up a picture from his desk and showed Tommy a sepia photograph of a young man in uniform, "He saw the damage done to men's minds. He fixed up their bones and their bullet wounds and they seemed healed, but he knew they were not and yet he sent them back to the front. The one that truly upset him was a lad of eighteen. He had been shot twice and sent back twice. The third time he was shot my grandson patched him up. He said the bullet wound was nothing compared to the lad's mental state. He jumped at shadows, had night terrors and would slip into periods of depression where he seemed unaware of anything. My grandson knew he was not fit to fight, but the bullet wound healed and back he went. The last my grandson saw of him he shook his hand with a smile and joked that he hoped not to see him again. Two days later that young man shot himself in the head."

Dr Cutt put down the photograph. His hand trembled slightly.

"My grandson returned home a hero among his contemporaries for the number of soldiers he had been able to save and send back to the front line. However, he hated himself because he had seen men in agony, an agony he could not cure and he had done nothing. What none of us realised, not even my grandson himself, was that he too was carrying a war wound. January last year that wound got the better of him. He shot himself, just like his eighteen-year-old patient had. Since then I have put all my energies into studying shell-shock and other mental traumas. Trying to prevent similar tragedies befalling other young men. The war is still claiming victims you know."

Dr Cutt went silent for a moment.

"Let me help you Thomas." He said at last.

Tommy stared at his legs.

"Just a sedative?"

"To see what happens." Dr Cutt nodded.

"All right, let's try it."

Dr Cutt patted him on the arm.

"Don't let anyone ever say you are not a brave man." The doctor stood and went to get a vial from a cabinet.

Tommy closed his eyes and sighed. What on earth was he doing?

Chapter Five

"Colonel Brandt, I am so glad you could come." Clara welcomed the colonel into her house, "Tommy and Annie are out, which is just as well. I don't want them knowing about this just yet."

"What are you up to Clara?" Brandt asked, stripping his coat off and hanging it on a hook, followed by his hat, "Your message was rather cryptic."

Colonel Brandt had met Clara a few months back when she was solving the mystery of his late friend's disappearance. Since then Clara had rather adopted the lonely old colonel and he regularly came for Sunday lunch. He also happened to have trained as a doctor under his father, before joining the army.

"I have a body I want you to look at." Clara explained.

"Here?"

"It's complicated. I had to tell Annie to stay out of the dining room and she is most peeved with me."

"Surely a dead body should be with the police?"

"As I say colonel, it's complicated."

"Perhaps I better take a look." The colonel said, rubbing anxiously at his chin.

Clara started to open the dining room door.

"Tell me colonel, in-between exotic birds, did you perhaps find the time to take a peek at the House of

Curios?"

The colonel endeavoured not to blush at the mention of his faux pas; he still had visions of nubile flesh running through his mind. It had certainly been an experience.

"Ah, yes, I believe I did."

"Good, then you will have met Hepkaptut before." Clara pushed open the door and led the way inside.

King Hepkaptut was laid out on the dining room table, a neatly ironed linen table cloth between his blackened body and the polished wood. Clara had kept the blind at the window drawn in case anyone peered in, but a side window cast bright sunlight over the corpse. He looked just as desiccated as in his display case, but the sunshine added a leathery-ness to the texture of his pitch black skin.

"You recognise him?" Clara asked.

"The mummy from the fairground." Brandt gasped in astonishment, "What is he doing here?"

"He is on loan." Clara winked, "In any case, I suspect this gentleman is no more an ancient Egyptian than you or I."

"I don't know." Mused Brandt, "Seen a few of these mummies in my time. He certainly looks the part."

"Well that is why I asked you to stop by. I wondered if you might use your medical knowledge to examine Hepkaptut here and tell me what you can about him."

"Now Clara, I never finished my training as a doctor."

Clara smiled.

"I know, but you do have medical knowledge, and I can't convince the police to get involved in this case until I can demonstrate that this man before us was murdered, or at least that he was a perfectly healthy and very much alive individual until around fifteen years ago."

Colonel Brandt shook his head.

"Slow down a moment. You think this is a murder victim?"

"I even have a potential name for him, and it isn't Hepkaptut."

Colonel Brandt stared a long time at the mummy on the table. To his eyes it looked like a dozen other mummies he had seen over his many years in the army. He had spent time in Egypt and the locals were fond of digging up mummies from old tombs and hawking them to tourists. Mostly they were unwrapped so people could see the actual corpse and they all had a blackened, wizened appearance the same as Hepkaptut. Of course, there was no knowing that those said mummies being sold in the market were real either, there was no trusting foreigners.

"I suppose I could take a look."

"Thank you colonel." Clara moved to the far side of the mummy to give Brandt room.

The colonel donned his monocle and approached the corpse. He peered at the dark skin, amazed to see the fine imprint of pores still visible on the flesh.

"It's a remarkable thing, mummification." He scanned his eyes down over the sunken rib-cage and to the spindly legs, "Safe to say he is male."

"I had noticed those." Clara said with a wry smile.

The colonel found himself blushing again.

"Mummification does preserve everything." He coughed, "He doesn't appear to have any obvious breaks in his limbs."

The colonel moved around to the side of the table where Clara stood and peered closer at Hepkaptut's chest.

"That's interesting. Clara do you have a candle or lamp perhaps so I could take a closer look at this?"

Clara vanished from the room and returned with an old oil lamp. She placed it on a small occasional table and fetched matches from the mantelpiece. It burst into flame a little too enthusiastically and she adjusted the wick before bringing it over to Colonel Brandt.

"Could you cast light just over this spot here, please?" Brandt motioned to the place on the chest he meant with his finger.

Clara leaned the lamp over as far as she dared, too

aware that she could spill hot oil on the tinder-dry mummy and incinerate them all. That would hardly be a fitting way to end a Tuesday morning. Oblivious to her concerns, Brandt stretched his head down until his nose was almost touching the body and peered through his monocle. After a moment he took it off and used it as a magnifying glass.

"Well I never. I do believe we have a bullet hole."

"Really?" Clara tried to look around Brandt's head.

"Yes. You see? It's a small hole about the size of a pencil and I would swear I could see something glinting inside it. Perhaps the bullet itself."

"Then my next question has to be, did this kill him?"

Brandt pulled his head back sharply, almost knocking the lamp out of Clara's hands in the process.

"I'm not expert enough to tell you. For all I know someone at the fairground took a pot-shot at old Hepkaptut one night. But a bullet wound is still a bullet wound."

"Anything else?"

Brandt returned his monocle to his eye and took a good look at the pharaoh's head.

"I suppose it is quite interesting his jaw is hanging open. I hadn't thought of that before, but most of the genuine mummies you see in places like the British museum have closed mouths."

"The jaw drops after death when the muscles release from rigor." Clara said with a nod, "I was a nurse in the war and I went into the morgue at the hospital more times than I care to remember. If you don't tie the jaw up then the mouth will flop open, like this."

"The ancient Egyptians were very precise about the appearance of their mummies, they wouldn't have liked that."

"So let's rule out the possibility this fellow was deliberately mummified for either strange funerary purposes or to fake a mummy, because the jaw would most likely have been held closed by some means until the process was done."

"Accidental mummification?"

"A murderer hides the body of his victim in a place conducive to such a process, then years later the corpse is discovered and mistaken for a much older body? It explains things as well as any other theory I have."

Brandt leaned over the corpse again.

"Two silver fillings." He said, "And a gold crown. Nice work, actually."

"Somehow I don't think that is the work of an ancient Egyptian dentist."

"No." Colonel Brandt stood upright and stretched his back. There was a faint crack, "Now what Clara?"

"I keep poking my nose around while also trying to convince the police they need to investigate this as a murder." Clara gave a shrug as if the task were simple, "One final question, do you see this ring on his hand?"

Clara pointed out the large ring Oliver had identified as belonging to Mervin Grimes.

"That looks valuable to me, but no one put in any effort to remove it. Any thoughts on why?"

Brandt used his monocle as a magnifier again.

"I would say they couldn't. From the look of the knuckle that ring has been worn for so long that the finger has swollen with age and would have made it impossible to remove without cutting it. In actual fact there is a mark in the skin here as if someone tried cutting off the finger but the tool wasn't sharp or strong enough and they gave up."

"Perhaps the killer had only limited time to dispose of the corpse and couldn't waste it on the ring." Clara theorised, "At least that also confirms that this ring was not placed on the mummy after death."

"Oh no, this ring has always been here." Brandt agreed, "He probably started to wear it as a young man and the finger grew. Bit like when an old woman tries to remove the wedding ring she wore as a girl. She can't get it over the knuckle because her hands have changed."

"Then I am satisfied this is the one and only Mervin Grimes." Clara perched her hands on her hips and stared at the body, "What a way to end your days."

"You know who he was?"

"Only vaguely. A thug who ran with some of the criminal gangs that haunt Brighton. Presumably he fell foul of someone."

"Clara, I don't want to preach, but do you really want to involve yourself in a gangster's death? These are dangerous people."

"It was fifteen years ago, the culprit may even be dead or in prison already."

"But supposing they are not and they don't want to be found?"

Clara cast her eye over the body of Mervin Grimes.

"No murderer wants to be found."

"Yes, but these fellows are very dangerous and they are not afraid of getting their hands dirty."

"I didn't say I was going to mix with them, as soon as I have enough pieces of the puzzle put together I shall just hand it over to the police and let them take charge."

"Good, because you owe Mervin Grimes nothing. He was a thug who ended up the way most thugs do, well, aside from the mummification."

Clara gave Colonel Brandt a smile.

"I think I owe you a cup of tea."

"That would be nice."

"I think Annie has made some currant cake, if we can find it."

"That sounds delightful." Colonel Brandt was almost at the dining room door when he paused and glanced back at Mervin.

"What is it like sleeping in a house with a mummy downstairs?" He asked.

Clara grinned at him.

"Quiet as a tomb." She said with a twinkle in her eye.

Chapter Six

Tommy was wheeled back into the waiting room to allow the sedative to take effect. Dr Cutt invited his next patient to come to his surgery before leaving Tommy to meditate on their conversation. Tommy gave a small sigh and looked at the coffee table in the middle of the room which was stacked with magazines. He reached forward to pick up a copy of the Brighton Gazette but the table was just out of reach. He cursed his legs as he stretched out again, his hand still falling short.

"Here, let me." A woman moved from her seat on his left and picked up the magazine. She handed it to him.

"Thank you." Tommy smiled, remembering that the woman had been in the room before he had gone in to see Dr Cutt. She was looking at him with a strange intensity.

"Excuse me, but did the doctor say you are Mr Thomas Fitzgerald?"

"Yes." Tommy tried to identify the woman's accent, it was faint but discernible and he had heard such an accent before.

Slowly the thought in his mind formed into the idea that the accent was German. Tommy's stomach sunk a little. For the last three years he had thrown all his bile and hate at Germany and anything with Teutonic overtones. Others had forgotten so fast, returning to their

German operas and novels, but Tommy had found it impossible to be so forgiving. To this day anything German made his stomach recoil in dozens of knots, his chest to tighten and an overwhelming feeling of rage take hold of his senses. All of a sudden he couldn't look the woman in the face. He supposed it was not her fault she was German, but just that faint hint of an accent had his teeth grinding and some inner demon clawing up his throat.

"I'm sorry to impose on you like this but, are you the brother of Miss Clara Fitzgerald?"

Tommy forced out the answer as politely as he could.

"Yes."

"And, could you say how much she charges for her services?"

Tommy still couldn't look at her face. He wanted to say some ridiculous price, send the woman away so she wouldn't bother them further. But some shred of decency ousted that irrational thought. After all it was up to Clara to decide who she would take on as a client, even if they were German.

"It... it depends really. On the case."

The woman suddenly took the seat next to him. It wasn't so much as if she had chosen to sit down, but rather that she had collapsed into it from exhaustion. She gave a long sigh, then opened her black handbag and withdrew a silver watch.

"The pawnbroker says this is worth £2. Would she accept this for her helping me?"

She placed the watch in Tommy's hands without another word. He looked at the beautiful watch, its enamel white face cut away at the top to reveal a hint of the intricate workings. Its case was ornamented with a pattern of flowers and vines and in the middle of the back was an engraving in German with two sets of initials intertwined. It was a fine watch and worth far more than £2.

"My late husband made it." The woman said quietly,

"You don't like Germans much, do you?"

Her comment took Tommy off-guard and jerked him from his thoughts.

"I..."

"It doesn't matter. Over the last six years I have seen it so much I hardly think about it now. That is why I noticed how your face changed when you heard my accent."

Tommy swallowed down on the choking anger before he replied.

"This watch is worth far more than £2." He forced himself to look her in the face. When he did he saw an older woman, whose round, homely face was much marked by time and worry. Her hair had mostly gone completely to grey, but a darkness at the roots suggested it had once been the deepest of blacks. She had probably never been pretty in the traditional sense, but her eyes had a sparkle, even if it was dulled with time, and there was a hint of a dimple in her cheek that would blossom when she smiled. She was dressed in dark blue and black, the style at least a decade out-of-date, and she looked so very, very sad.

"I'm so sorry." Tommy said quietly.

"I told you it doesn't matter."

"I think it does." Tommy ran his finger over the front of the watch, "Your husband was very skilled. This is a fine piece."

He drew out his own English pocket-watch for comparison, the one his father had had for years. It looked cumbersome and workman-like next to the delicate silver watch.

"My husband made watches since he was fourteen. He learnt from his father in Prussia. We came to London in 1897 and there we set up a shop. He made watches for gentlemen and was very proud of the fact."

"I can see why he would be popular." Tommy handed back the watch.

"Until the war." The woman smiled sadly, "Then he

was just another German and no one wanted his watches. It would be unpatriotic. No matter we had been in England for seventeen years and that my son spoke with a London accent. He was only three when we came to England. He has never been to Germany."

She toyed with the watch.

"I don't blame people. We came to Brighton and changed our surname to Smith. My husband spent his time mending watches rather than making them, but at least it was work." She slipped the watch back into her bag, "I'm sorry, I am rambling."

Tommy gave her a genuine smile.

"That's all right." He said, "My sister would not like you to pawn that watch just to pay her, you know. Perhaps if you explain why you need her help I could give you a better idea of what she would charge?"

Mrs Smith stared at her handbag for a moment. When she looked up her eyes were teary.

"It's my son. He is missing. Has been for the last two years." She opened the bag again and pulled out a photograph of a young man, "His name is Jurgen. He will be 26 next month."

She handed over the photograph which was about the size of a visiting card and showed a youth with dark hair and a shy smile. He wore a suit and was leaning against a low brick wall, his head half turned from the camera as if caught by surprise.

"Did he serve in the war?" Tommy asked with that knot in his throat again. In his mind Jurgen Smith's suit was replaced by the spiked helmet and grey uniform of the German army.

"Jurgen would have loved to serve in the British army. You mistake me, Mr Fitzgerald, I did not favour Germany in the war. Neither I nor my husband could see the point in conflict. It was why we left Prussia in the first place. Jurgen was patriotic to King George and would have given his life for England in an instant if he had had the chance. Only Germans, even Germans who thought of themselves as British, were not allowed in the king's army."

"Then, what happened to him?"

"In 1914 we received a letter explaining that the government was interning British Germans as part of its war policies. I suppose they thought some of us might be spies or saboteurs. I cried when I read it." Mrs Smith took back the photograph and a tear trickled down her face unheeded, "My son and my husband were both to be interned, but my husband was very ill with his chest and could barely walk. So we managed to get him excused as he clearly could do little harm to anyone. But Jurgen had to go. They sent him away to the Isle of Man just before Christmas."

Mrs Smith began to rummage in her bag again.

"He was interned for four years, but he wrote often, and he knew about our move to Brighton. He said he was looking forward to seeing the new house. I carry the last letter I received from him with me all the time." She removed a much-read letter from her bag, the corners were worn away and the paper was starting to rip down the creases, "He sent me this in December 1918, just before he was due to come home."

Tommy was handed the letter and he read, with a little difficulty, the tightly packed writing on the page.

"Dear mum and dad,

Good news! I am due to get the next ferry across to England, then I will be on the train and headed home. It's been a long time. Some of the men here are resentful about being imprisoned, I tell them it can't have been as bad as those filthy trenches in France, so they should cheer up. It hasn't been a bad time, don't think we had it rough. This isn't a prison, but I do miss London and you. I keep thinking about what I shall do once I am home. I still have my heart set on training in engineering, perhaps I can find a course or something when I get back? I hear that with so many dead and injured they are going to need a lot of new lads to fill jobs, so maybe I should just apply for something. Anyway, we can discuss that when I get home. Not long now! I have a Christmas present for you, but don't get too excited, it isn't much, just a token. Something I've worked on over the years. I'm running late for the post, so I better finish up here.

Take care of yourselves
See you soon
Your loving son, Jurgen"

"But he never arrived?" Tommy handed back the letter.

"No. I waited and waited. I was in a dreadful turmoil, you see, because I had never explained about his father." Mrs Smith bit her lip, "Jurgen's father took the war hard. We changed our name, but somehow we were still German, still the enemy. He was a proud man, but very sensitive. I think in the end he felt so ashamed of the way Germany had behaved and therefore he felt ashamed of being German. He was very honourable. Germans are. He took his honour seriously and it pained him to see what his countrymen were doing in the name of Germany. One day that shame overcame everything else. I found him in his workshop, the gun he had shot himself with still in his hand."

Tommy's stomach turned over. In just half an hour that was the third person he had heard about who had shot themselves because of the war. It was disquieting and made him all the more relieved his own pistol was a useless relic, its workings clogged with Flanders mud. There had been a point where, had it been in working order, it might have provided a tempting answer to his own anguish.

"You did not tell Jurgen?"

"It's not the sort of news you write in a letter and, well..." Mrs Smith grimaced, "I couldn't face explaining it, not then. And the longer I left it, the harder it was to think about writing it down on paper. I should have told him, I intended to. I just didn't."

"I can see these last few years have been hard on you Mrs Smith."

Mrs Smith gave a hollow laugh.

"Very hard. I turn up an hour early for a doctor's appointment just to avoid being in the house alone."

"My sister has worked on a lot of missing person cases, she might be able to help."

"I don't expect Jurgen to be alive. I hope, naturally. But if he was alive he would have come home. I just need to know what happened to him."

Tommy nodded.

"Look, my sister will gladly accept whatever you can afford. Don't pawn the watch or anything else."

"Thank you. That is the kindest thing anyone has done for me in years." Mrs Smith almost cried. Her relief was palpable.

"Just give me your address and the relevant details about Jurgen. His date of birth, height, German name, and any details about exactly where he was interned."

"I have all his letters and things. I could bring them to you?"

"That would be ideal." Tommy dug in his pocket and drew out a crumpled cigarette card featuring one of his favourite cricket players. He decided the card would have to be sacrificed in the name of a good cause, and borrowed a pencil off Mrs Smith to jot down the Fitzgerald home address, "I'll be in all tomorrow, thought I can't guarantee Clara will be."

"Thank you very much, I will drop by in the morning."

Mrs Smith carefully put the card away in her bag.

"And thank you Mr Fitzgerald for talking to a German."

Tommy suddenly felt ashamed of his earlier reaction to the woman.

"I shouldn't... I mean, it's not your fault the war began." He stammered.

"But I saw how hard it was for you, because of what you went through. I can understand that. I didn't say it to make you feel bad, just to let you know that I appreciate your patience with me when it must be difficult."

"The war left a lot of… unpleasant feelings." Tommy explained.

"As long as you can accept I am not the enemy?" Mrs Smith gave him a gentle smile, "I will look forward to seeing you tomorrow."

Dr Cutt appeared around the door at that moment.

"Mr Fitzgerald? How are the legs?" He asked merrily.

Tommy found he had not been paying attention to the effects of the sedative. He rubbed at his thigh.

"A little numb. In fact, I feel a bit numb all over."

"Good! Time for the next phase." He went to grab Tommy's chair, "Good morning Mrs Schmitt, you're early."

Mrs Smith/Schmitt nodded her head at him.

"Now Thomas, I want you to clear your mind of all thoughts." Dr Cutt continued as he pushed Tommy from the room.

Tommy realised he had not been listening, his mind instead turned to wondering what had become of the young Jurgen.

"Hmm?"

"Clear your mind of all thoughts."

"Oh, right." Tommy pulled a face. He might as well have been asked to stand up and tap dance. Oh well, it was just one more experiment to prove he couldn't walk. Tommy tried to block out thoughts of Jurgen Smith and his lonely mother. Whatever had become of him it was Clara's mystery to solve.

Only problem was he couldn't help an image of that silver watch flashing back into his mind, and the sensitive, ill man behind it who had shot himself out of shame for being German. Somehow he just knew there was a tragedy lurking in the background of the Smith life, one that had yet to be discovered and he had the nasty feeling he was going to be the one to do it.

Chapter Seven

'Mummification methods' was one of those topics the Brighton library card catalogue did not appear to cover. Clara found this highly annoying, but she was not deterred and a visit to the local rare bookseller's shop provided her with a volume from 1878 on the processes used by the ancient Egyptians. She read it while sipping tea and consuming cucumber sandwiches in a nearby teashop. The author, a member of the landed gentry turned Egyptian scholar, had spent many years exploring the old tombs of the pharaohs. He had experimented to produce his own mummies and demonstrate how the Egyptians had done it. All this work had then been combined into a rather heavy-handed text that explained in 200 pages what exactly mummification was. Filtering out the worst excesses of the author's bad prose, Clara found herself learning that the main components for mummification were heat and a lack of moisture. Early Egyptian corpses had merely been buried in the dry sands of the desert and this had effected the process, though not as well as the later techniques devised by the embalmers. Even today animals and even people were sometimes found mummified in the dry heat of Egypt.

Closer to home, though mummification was rarer in temperate climates, it was not unheard of. The author cited the many finds of mummified cats in wall cavities. These unfortunate creatures had perhaps climbed into the space between two walls after a mouse and become trapped. The insulating nature of the gap, perhaps combined by the warmth of a nearby fireplace dried them out rapidly and caused the tiny bodies to be mummified. This gave Clara her first idea of how Mervin Grimes had come to be so oddly preserved. He clearly had not been in a desert, but perhaps his body had been concealed in a wall, somewhere warm, and by chance he had become a mummy.

Clara dredged another cup of tea out of the teapot and mused on her findings. What were the odds the killer had deliberately intended Mervin's corpse to become mummified? For that matter, where would he have gotten the idea? Gangsters were not renowned for their intellectual prowess, so would one of them have even thought about mummification as a means of disguising a corpse? Equally, there was no obvious reason for how Mervin had ended up as a fairground attraction, unless it really was a case of the murderer hiding the corpse in plain sight. Clara's mind went back to the break-in the other night. Was that coincidence or something else?

Whatever it was, it really was time Clara paid a visit to the police.

Clara strolled down the road to the police station, carrying her new book under one arm. Life, she mused to herself, could be very peculiar sometimes. She found her least favourite desk sergeant on duty and gave him her brightest smile. Clara's theory was that all miserable people had a breaking point, if you just kept on being nice and jolly to them eventually they would crack and smile back.

"Good afternoon, might I speak to Inspector Park-Coombs?"

The desk sergeant glowered at her.

"Miss Fitzgerald, isn't it?"

"Quite right. Is the inspector in?"

The sergeant huffed.

"Is he expecting you?"

"I couldn't say." Clara answered vaguely, "He's a perceptive man after all, and it is entirely possible he witnessed me walking here from a window."

"What?" The desk sergeant stared at her with a hint of annoyed bemusement.

"I said he might be expecting me, but the odds are he is not."

Her attempt at light-hearted banter earned nothing more than a stern stare.

"If you haven't got an appointment I can't do anything."

"Stop right there sergeant, now surely you have known me long enough to realise I don't wander into police stations on idle business. I have a suspicious death to report and I think the inspector would like to hear about it."

"I have a form for that." The desk sergeant said stiffly, he reached under his desk and produced a thick folder. With irritating slowness he thumbed through its contents, "Here it is, form 190. Suspicious death of person or persons."

"I would much prefer to speak to the inspector in person."

"That you might, but this is how we do things around here."

Clara caught herself before she lost her temper. Since her first introduction to the world of Brighton crime, her bane had been the paperwork-obsessed police who barred her way at every turn. Despite proving to them on at least two occasions that she was not an idle gossip or busybody, they still caused her all manner of bother whenever she tried to report a crime.

"This won't do sergeant. I must speak to the inspector."

"Name?" The sergeant licked his pencil and hovered it over the form.

"Clara Fitzgerald."

"Named of deceased, if known?"

"Mervin Grimes, look sergeant…"

"Reason for believing the victim to have died under suspicious circumstances?"

Clara gave a sigh.

"He has a bullet wound in his chest."

The sergeant gave her an odd look.

"And where did you see this body?"

"Last time I checked he was on my dining room table." Clara was pleased to see a spasm of shock cross the desk sergeant's face, "Oh, and he was mummified. Do you have a section on your form for that?"

The desk sergeant put down his pencil.

"I think you ought to see the inspector?"

"Really?" Clara beamed her brightest smile, "Because there is clearly more form to fill in as yet."

The desk sergeant rang a bell on his desk and a constable appeared from a back room.

"Take this lady to inspector Park-Coombs office." He ordered, "But don't let her out of your sight."

"Thank you sergeant." Clara said as she went to follow the constable.

The desk sergeant gave another huff, then started ripping up his defaced suspicious deaths form.

"Mummified indeed!" He puttered.

Inspector Park-Coombs had just refilled his teacup and was inspecting the tin in his top desk drawer for biscuits when the constable tapped on his door and presented Clara. Park-Coombs gave a sigh and shut the drawer.

"Miss Fitzgerald, did you have a good holiday?"

"Mostly, aside from the murder."

"Yes, I heard about that. Rather attract them, don't you?"

Clara gave him an offended look.

"Just don't take a holiday around May time in Blackpool, that's when me and the missus like to go there. I would rather not have a murder to solve when I am trying to relax."

"I don't go looking for murders, you know." Clara said, taking the chair in front of Park-Coombs' desk even though he had failed to offer it.

"Certainly not, they just seem to have a knack of finding you. Anyway, what is this all about?"

"I am quite hurt inspector, I might almost consider not telling you what I came here for."

"Then again…" The inspector took a sip of tea.

Clara, who was neither hurt nor offended, knew not to take the inspector too seriously. She rested her elbows on the desk and gave him a grin.

"You already know about this one."

"Do I?"

"Yes, because Oliver Bankes reported it, but there was not enough evidence for the police to do anything."

The inspector gave this some thought.

"I don't recall Mr Bankes reporting a crime."

"It probably went through that desk sergeant downstairs." Clara pulled a face, "He still thinks I am a nuisance."

Park-Coombs raised his eyebrows, as if to imply he wasn't too sure he didn't agree with the desk sergeant on that. Clara wisely chose to ignore him.

"I have a mummified corpse lying on my dining room table at home."

"Really?"

"Really." Clara carried on before the inspector was distracted too much by that thought, "His name was Mervin Grimes. He died around fifteen years ago and somehow his body became mummified. This is where things get puzzling. His mummified corpse ended up in a fairground attraction called the House of Curios, where Oliver spotted him."

Inspector Park-Coombs stretched backwards in his chair, his face a contortion of confusion.

"We are sure this is a real body?"

"Yes."

"The real body of Mervin Grimes?"

"Yes, he still bears a personalised ring he always wore. His killer couldn't get it off his hand. Oliver has a picture of Mervin showing him wearing that ring. I'm sure, if necessary, we could find other proof. He had some nice dentistry work for instance, perhaps we could find his dentist?"

"Definitely murdered?"

"I'm fairly confident. There is a bullet hole in his chest, though of course it might be post-mortem. Only your coroner might be able to say for certain."

Inspector Park-Coombs whistled softly through his moustache. He was starting to feel the need for something much stronger than just tea.

"That name, Mervin Grimes, rings a bell." He stood and went to the wooden filing cabinet by his window. He opened a drawer and ran a finger through a set of cardboard folders stored under the letter G, "Fifteen years ago I had just been made an inspector."

He pulled out a folder and brought it across to the desk.

"Ah yes, Mervin Grimes, petty criminal. Lowest of the low, in my opinion. Ran with the Black Hand gang. Usual stuff, fixing races, drug dealing, prostitution. Mervin was a bit handy with a knife and too quick with his temper. We never caught him, but we were closing in when he vanished. Around 1905 a big deal went down at the racetrack. A filly staked at 200 to 1 romped home and won. Needless to say people were suspicious, doping was suspected. Mervin and other members of the Black Hand went home with bulging pockets, which only confirmed our suspicions. Nothing we could do though. Quite frankly I was rather glad when this Grimes fellow vanished. About the same time the Black Hand disbanded and the members all went their merry ways."

"Does that mean you are not interested that he is dead?"

"Not really. It solved a problem. So one criminal killed

another? In the scheme of things that makes my life easier and I have far too many crimes involving law abiding citizens to want to waste my time on a criminal who wound up dead." The inspector tapped a thick forefinger on the folder, "This is one to stay out of Clara."

"Whatever the nature of the man, he was murdered."

"Stay out of it. Criminals kill each other all the time. Sometimes we nab the killer, a lot of times we don't."

Clara appreciated the inspector's sentiments, but she also knew Oliver was not going to let this rest, and she also suspected she would find it difficult to sleep at night until she had settled the tragedy of Mervin Grimes. Whoever he was in life, his corpse told a pretty depressing tale. Murdered and then presented as a carnival attraction. However you looked at it that was not a very respectful way to treat the dead. Mervin might have been a thug, but if you only meted out justice to the righteous what sort of person did that make you? What sort of society? Clara fully understood the inspector had more cases than he had time to solve them in, and he had to pick and choose which occupied him the most. But that was not the same with her. If she turned down Mervin Grimes' case, what was her excuse other than she couldn't care less about a dead thug? Clara felt that would make her a pretty poor detective.

"Does that folder mention next of kin?"

"Clara, this is not a case you want to involve yourself in." Park-Coombs was pleading now.

"I just wondered if there was a family who might like to know what became of Mervin. Maybe even to bury him."

Park-Coombs knew that wasn't the full story, but couldn't argue with her compassion. He flicked open the folder and then wrote out a name and address on a slip of paper.

"His mother. Don't get into trouble." He said as he handed it over.

"The man has been dead 15 years, what trouble could

there be?" Clara slipped the paper into her handbag, "Does that file say what the police thought had happened to Mervin?"

"I think official opinion was that he had gone to London. We reported this to the boys at Scotland Yard, just in case he caused his usual brand of trouble in the Capital and left it at that. Gangs are part and parcel of Brighton and there are plenty more thugs where Mervin Grimes came from."

"Never mind inspector, you do your best."

"Thank you." The inspector answered the double-edged compliment through gritted teeth.

"I shall be on my way again, but I don't suppose I could impose on your coroner to remove Mervin Grimes' corpse from my dining room to his morgue? At least until I find out what the family want to do."

The inspector gave a funny snort.

"I'll give him a call. Perhaps he can pop around this afternoon?" There was a snide hint to his tone.

"Very good inspector, I'll expect him after 3 o'clock, if you don't mind." Clara was at the door, one hand on the handle.

"I don't mind at all. Now Clara," Park-Coombs paused her as she was about to leave, "Take care, all right."

Clara was touched by his concern and gave him a smile.

"I always do inspector." And then she was gone, back on her mission to solve the death of a gangster.

Chapter Eight

Clara caught an omnibus headed in the direction of West street, aiming to speak to Mervin Grimes' mother before she went home. If his mother still lived at that address, of course. West Street was a long line of small terraces, one end being slightly smarter and more upmarket than the other. There was even a policeman or two living in the better part of West street, but the other part, the part where houses jostled each other's shoulders and doors opened straight onto the road, was only a few steps up from a slum. Yes the doorsteps were clean and the windows mostly sparkled, but it would not take much for many of the families living in these houses to find themselves unable to pay the rent and headed for the darker, grimmer parts of town where children played without shoes and rubbish collected in heaps in the gutters.

Clara alighted at this end of the road and located number 68, the home of Sarah Grimes, mother of the infamous Mervin. Clara took a moment to survey the front of the house before knocking on the door. Fronts of houses could tell you a lot about the owner. This one was clean, but without the ornamentation some of the neighbours had tried to brighten their living spaces. There was no box of flowers on the windowsill like at 66, or a hand-carved wooden boot scraper as outside number 70. The front window displayed an empty glass vase, but no flourish of bric-a-brac as in the window of number 64. The whole appearance gave Clara the impression of sadness, a house where the basics were tended to, to keep it smart, but where anything beyond that was just too much. Clara wondered if the person within would confirm her assessment.

She rapped on the door. There was no knocker. It was a long while before anyone answered.

"Yes?"

"Are you Mrs Sarah Grimes?"

"Yes?"

Mrs Grimes was younger than Clara had expected. Imagining that Mervin would now be about 35, she had expected Mrs Grimes to be well into her fifties, instead she was probably only in her forties. Her hair was still auburn and barely streaked with grey. With it tied back in a plait she almost looked school-girlish. Her eyes were a deep brown and only showing the first signs of crow's-feet, her face was narrow, ending in a sharp chin that jutted out a little and gave the impression of petulance. She could not have been more than five foot tall and Clara had to look down at her.

"Might I come in Mrs Grimes? I have some news about your son."

Clara had not expected much of a response from the woman and she wasn't disappointed. Mrs Grimes merely gave a nod.

"This way then." She led Clara into a narrow hall and into the second room down where a broad-shouldered gentleman was sitting squashed into a floral armchair that barely contained his girth.

"All right Mrs Grimes?" He asked suspiciously as Clara entered, putting down a dainty cup and saucer that looked straight out of a child's tea set in his hands.

"This lady says she has news on Mervin." Sarah Grimes said in a dull voice. She sat down in another armchair without looking at Clara.

"Clara Fitzgerald." Clara held out her hand to the large gentleman.

He shook it after a moment's thought.

"Bob Waters." He introduced himself, "What is this about Mervin?"

"Were you a friend?" Clara asked cautiously, aware that anyone in Mervin's circle of acquaintances could be his killer.

"His oldest friend." Bob said staunchly, a hint of pride in his tone.

Clara wondered if she was facing one of the former Black Hand gang.

"I'm afraid the news I have to tell you is not good." Clara said carefully.

"He's dead." Sarah Grimes said flatly, "I've known that for the past 15 years. My Mervin wouldn't up and leave me unless he couldn't help it."

"He disappeared suddenly?" Clara asked.

It was Bob that answered.

"Just gone overnight. Not a word. I always said it was foul doings. He ran with a bad lot, did Mervin."

Clara decided to chance her luck.

"With the Black Hand gang."

"Yeah, how you know that?" Bob said in surprise.

"I hear things." Clara shrugged, "Were you a member too, Bob?"

Bob gave her a lopsided grin.

"Not on your life. My ma would have skinned me alive if I had joined them, God rest her soul. Not that I'm a saint mind." Bob winked.

"My Mervin never knew how to keep out of trouble." Sarah Grimes sighed heavily, "Ever since he could walk he was into mischief. I didn't know about the gang till after he was gone. Knew he was in trouble, that's all. After he vanished I had all these mean-looking fellows hammering at my door after him. If it hadn't been for Bob I don't know what I would have done."

Bob gave a gesture that implied he hardly could not help his best friend's mother.

"Done a bit of boxing in my time." He said, clenching up his fists, "Best fight is always after the match when the losing punters try to take on the winning ones and anyone else who happens to be in the way."

Clara found herself warming to Bob and his enormous frame.

"Pity Mervin didn't stick with you Bob." Sarah said quietly.

"Ah, he never had any sense, you know that." Bob grimaced, "So what's the news you have brought us Miss Fitzgerald."

"It's a tad complicated, but I think I have found his body."

Sarah Grimes gave a little start, but Bob merely looked sad.

"After all this time?" Sarah said, "Where?"

"I'm sorry to say in the fairground."

"The one on the seafront?" Bob looked puzzled, "What was he doing there? If he was back in Brighton why didn't he come to see his old mum?"

"I didn't explain myself well." Clara apologised, "He has been dead these fifteen years, but his body was recently found in the fairground. It is a tad unpleasant, but it appears Mervin was mummified."

Bob looked blank.

"What's that mean?" He said.

"Like ancient Egyptian mummies." Clara explained, "It's a very strange thing."

"Miss Fitzgerald," Sarah Grimes spoke up, her voice tight, "Perhaps you could explain what you have to do with my son at all. What is it any of your business how he died?"

Bob looked away at the sharpness of Mrs Grimes' tone, perhaps thinking he had been too cheerful and chatty under the circumstances. Clara wasn't sure how to explain her presence concisely, she was also very aware that she had not been offered a seat or a cup of tea. Either Mrs Grimes was a neglectful hostess or Clara's visit was deeply unwanted. She suspected the latter.

"I was asked to identify the body." Clara finally said, withdrawing a card from her purse and handing it first to Sarah Grimes.

"Haven't got me glasses on." Sarah wrinkled her nose, "And these squiggly letters people print stuff in make my eyes go queer."

She gave the card to Bob, almost throwing it at him. Bob held it as close to his nose as it was feasible to get. Clara wondered he wasn't going cross-eyed trying to read it at that distance.

"Pri-vate de-tec-tive." He read carefully, before passing the card back to Clara.

"You see, the body was spotted by someone who suspected it was that of Mervin Grimes. But it wasn't clear, so they asked me to track down evidence that it really was Mervin before proceeding further."

"Why didn't they just come to me?" Sarah Grimes puttered, "I'm his mother, ain't I? I could have told 'em if it was Mervin."

"I'm afraid Mrs Grimes that mummification makes a body difficult to recognise. However Mervin was wearing a large ring marked with what appear to be an S, beneath a domed piece of sapphire. It was from that we identified him."

"That bloody thing." Mrs Grimes snorted, she was beginning to lose her earlier indifference and instead sounded very angry, "He won a little on the dogs when he was sixteen and bought himself this ring. Tawdry little bauble it was, but he thought it made him seem quite the gent. He never took it off. Oh my poor Mervin."

Sarah Grimes sniffed and stared away into the small fireplace

"What happens now, miss?" Bob asked sadly, "Are the police going to come calling."

"The police…" Clara hesitated, tact was called for,

"believe that after such a long time it will be virtually impossible to find the killer."

"You mean they don't care because my Mervin was a gangster." Mrs Grimes snapped, her tears no longer in evidence, "Well he was a gangster, but a good lad too. He never done any real harm. But the police don't care tuppence for that, do they? Just another one they don't have to worry about."

"I'm sorry Mrs Grimes, really I am." Clara almost reached out to the women, then thought better of the gesture, she still felt unwelcome in the house, "At least now Mervin can have a decent burial."

"Hah!" Mrs Grimes glared at her, "Decent? On what little money I have? You must be out of your mind. And I suppose you want to charge me for this little visit too, Miss Fitzgerald, private detective?"

"This was purely courtesy."

"Or bloody nosiness! Do you think I need you coming around here telling me my son is dead? Do you think I am too stupid to realise that after all these years? Swanning in, in all your fancy clothes, looking down at my little humble home. Does it make you feel better to know a gangster's mum is virtually destitute? Crime doesn't pay and all that, bet the police are having a good laugh over my son's body!"

"That's enough Mrs Grimes." Bob stood from his chair; his size suddenly became even more pronounced as he filled the whole room with his broad, thick shoulders, "That's enough. I'll see Miss Fitzgerald out. You need to start thinking what you want doing with poor Mervin's body."

"And what will I do, hey?" Mrs Grimes had started to sob, thick tears rolled down her cheeks, "Can't even bury my only son properly. Oh the shame of it."

"Come on." Bob gently took Clara's elbow, "Once she starts like this it will be hours before I can talk sense to her again."

He led Clara into the cramped hall, which only just

seemed wide enough for him, and opened the front door. Clara stepped back into the fresh air and sunlight, rather relieved to be out of the oppressive atmosphere of the Grimes' house.

"You have to excuse Mervin's mum." Bob hovered on the doorstep uncomfortably, "She hasn't been right since Mervin vanished. Never really got over it. He was the only thing she had, what with Mr Grimes leaving them when Mervin was only a little boy. They never had much money. That's why Mervin got into crime in the first place."

"I've very sorry to hear that." Clara said politely.

"That night Mervin just disappeared, that was hard. Things were just starting to go right for 'em. Mervin had won a good bit of money on the horses, I don't say it was legal, but when you is that poor you don't really care. Anyway, last I see Mervin he is wearing a new bowler and is taking his mum out for a slap-up meal. Mrs Grimes was all a dither, like they say, giddy as a schoolgirl, that was her. Mervin turns to me as they were going out and says 'this is the start of new things Bob, me mum's going to be all right now.' And the next day he was gone."

"Do you suppose it was another gangster who murdered him?"

"Who knows." Bob shrugged those huge shoulders, nearly taking out the door frame in the process, "It was a lot of money Mervin won. Maybe he screwed someone over for it. I don't know, as I say I was never into that stuff."

"Oh well, thank you anyway Bob." Clara turned onto the pavement, "Give Mrs Grimes my regards when she calms down."

She had walked a few paces away, thinking what a sorry world some people lived in, when she heard a heavy footstep behind her. Bob had caught her up.

"Look, I can't pay you or nothing, but…" Bob looked agitated, he was shifting his weight from foot-to-foot, "you and I know the police have no interest in finding who killed Mervin Grimes, they are just glad he is dead. But I would like to know and his mum would too. I remember Mervin before the bad stuff, he was a good friend. I owe him for that. I could do some work for you to pay the bill, I'm employed as a carpenter."

Clara gave Bob a smile.

"I will see what I can dig up, but I don't expect payment."

"No?"

"Sometimes I am just nosy." Clara gave a wink, then she turned away and headed for the nearest omnibus stop.

"If you need anything just ask." Bob called after her, "You know where to find me."

He scuffed his feet on the ground, wondering if he had done the right thing. As an after-thought he shouted out.

"And do be careful!"

Chapter Nine

Tommy pressed the tips of his fingers together, braced his elbows on the table and rested his chin on the platform his hands had formed. He had spent a lot of time thinking about the war in the last few hours – dark, unhappy thoughts. Dr Cutt had felt there were signs for optimism when Tommy returned to his surgery after the sedative. He had blindfolded him and then run through a series of tests to see how much or little Tommy's legs were working. He felt the results had been promising, though for Tommy the consultation had seemed to consist of pins being shoved into his toes. In any case he had to go back in a week's time.

Had he not had the diversion of Mrs Smith to occupy his thoughts he might have found himself contemplating too hard on his doctor's appointment. As it was he had hardly given Dr Cutt a thought since he had left the surgery. The story of Jurgen Smith had completely absorbed his mind.

Tommy suspected that Jurgen was dead, how, where or why was another matter. Finding the answers to those questions would probably not bring Mrs Smith any peace, but it would be something. The question was, where to begin? He knew the last place Jurgen had been, but then what? If he had caught the ferry as he said, he would have come back to the mainland, then he must have had some plan as to how he was going to get home. Logically he would catch a train, perhaps overnight. So which train was he liable to catch? Tommy pulled down a book off a shelf, it was listed as a railway guide showing all the stations and tracks available in 1908, things could not have changed so much in twelve years, could they? Tommy flipped to the section listed as Isle of Man, and began making notes of all the trains which could carry a man to or from the ferry that served as a link to the island. After ruling out routes that were for goods trains, detracting smaller lines and ones that would lead in the opposite direction to Brighton, he had narrowed his options to four routes, each with a stop in London. If Jurgen Smith took any of these trains he would have found himself in the great city and just a stone's throw from a train that would take him home. So why had he never made it to Brighton?

An accident, was the logical answer, or possibly Jurgen was not the son Mrs Smith so dutifully remembered and he had decided to simply vanish. If that was the case tracing him would be virtually impossible. But whatever the cause, the only way to find out more was to contact the stations in question and see what records they saved about their passengers. He could get lucky, on the other hand it might be a dead end. He made a note of the name of the first station, then pushed his wheelchair into the hall and picked up the receiver of the phone. He asked the operator to connect him to Liverpool and then waited patiently as the phone rang and rang.

"Good afternoon, Liverpool Central Railway Station. Stationmaster Jones speaking." A slightly out-of-breath voice answered on the eighth ring.

"Ah, hello Mr Jones, I am making an enquiry on behalf of a friend about passengers who took your trains two years ago. More specifically German passengers coming from the Isle of Man and heading probably to London or Brighton."

"What a strange request." Mr Jones said over the phone, Tommy had visions of him as a gentleman with glasses and a moustache and one of those large railway pocket watches, "Why would they want to know that?"

"We are trying to trace someone who was once interned on the Isle," Tommy decided honesty was better than trying to think of a plausible lie, that was Clara's department, "He went missing shortly after sending word that he was coming home."

"Oh, I see. So you want to know if he caught a train here?"

"Yes, he was travelling under the name Jurgen Smith and it would have been the end of 1918, just before Christmas."

"I do recall a lot of Germans booking tickets about that time. Of course we knew a little about them being interned on the island. Smith, you say? Not very German."

"I believe they anglicised their name."

"I see, well if he was on this train there may be a record of it. During the war, because of espionage concerns, our head office decided we should take names of all passengers boarding our trains. I think we kept the books running until late 1918. I could check through them?"

"That would be most helpful, I am fully prepared to compensate you for your time. Perhaps you could send me a letter explaining whether you found anything or not?"

"I could, indeed, do that. Was this fellow a spy? I always wanted to catch one and be a hero."

"As far as I am aware he wasn't." Tommy answered as honestly as he could.

"Shame. But I'll do it anyway."

"Thank you Mr Jones." Tommy recited his house address over the phone and with a final expression of his gratitude to the helpful stationmaster he put down the receiver.

That happened to be the same moment Clara walked

in the door.

"Tommy, would you mind keeping Annie in the kitchen for a few minutes? Some men from the police are outside and I don't want her seeing what I'm about." Clara was pulling off her hat and gloves as she spoke.

"Is this to do with the mummified corpse on the dining room table?"

"You were not supposed to go in there!" Clara said in exasperation.

Tommy merely raised his eyebrows at her.

"Fine, it is about the mummy. Annie doesn't know?" Clara suddenly looked worried.

"I like Annie's cooking, so no, I didn't let her see what was decorating the dining table." Tommy gave his sister a grin, "She would run a mile if she knew."

"Which is why you will keep her in the kitchen." Clara said firmly.

"Absolutely."

There was a knock on the door and the police coroner poked his head into the hallway.

"Are we all right to come in? The police wagon outside is causing your neighbours some consternation." Dr Deáth (pronounced De-Ath) was a small, jolly man who did not give at first glance a hint that he spent all day working with dead people, many of whom had come to their untimely ends under unpleasant circumstances. In fact, he managed to make his morgue an almost welcoming place. But then, Clara supposed, why should one be miserable just because one was dead?

"Come in Dr Death. I would offer you tea but…"

"No, of course, let's get this over and done with swiftly. My lads have got the stretcher."

Clara led Dr Deáth into the dining room. Even as experienced as he was, Deáth gave a start at the sight of Mervin Grimes. His lads came very close to dropping the stretcher.

"What a fascinating case!" Dr Deáth peered over Mervin's head, "Everything preserved! Natural I would say, modern mummification like the Americans' use involves large amounts of chemicals and leaves the body flesh-coloured. Arsenic at one time was quite popular. In fact, I almost wondered if it was a poisoning case when I was told I was collecting a mummy. Arsenic victims are often remarkably preserved after years in the ground."

"Mervin was shot, we think." Clara pointed out the bullet hole.

"Indeed, I shall examine it and see if I can determine whether the bullet killed him. And you say he was just propped up in the fairground?"

"Displayed as an Egyptian pharaoh."

"How curious! I really should go to fairgrounds more often." Dr Deáth bent his head until he was almost nose to nose with Mervin's grimacing face, "You don't see this sort of thing often in England, we don't have the weather for it really. Too damp, you see. The ancient Egyptians used to remove all the bodily organs because they liquefy rapidly and encourage all sorts of insects that help the decaying process. Worst of all being the intestines, filled as they are with waste material. Yes, all told, this fellow was very lucky to have lasted in this way."

"I suspect he wouldn't agree." Clara said with a faint smile, "Nor his murderer for that matter."

"True, no murderer with any shred of sanity would want to see their victim on display." Deáth ran his fingers over the leather-like flesh of one of Mervin's arms, "Well, old chap, shall we get you back to my headquarters?"

He motioned to the two lads with the stretcher, who came forward with noticeable reluctance.

"You'll see a lot worse if you carry on working for me." Deáth puttered at their reticence, "Here, you get his feet, you his shoulders, I'll support the middle. And don't let anything drop off!"

Clara held her breath as the stiff mummy was manhandled off the table and deposited on the stretcher. No significant portion of Mervin Grimes fell off in the process, though he did leave quite a lot of dust and a few large flakes of black material on the table. Clara was inordinately glad she had put a cloth on the table before Mervin had taken residence there. She decided the linen cloth would have to be disposed of at once, there was simply no way she could reuse it after seeing it covered in bits of Mervin.

Deáth covered Mervin with a white cloth and ushered his stretcher-bearers to the door.

"Give me a day or two to take a better look at our fellow here and then pop by." Deáth grinned at Clara, "I'll make us a pot of tea when you come."

"You make it hard to resist." Clara laughed.

The body was negotiated out of the front door. Several of Clara's neighbours were on their doorsteps pretending not to notice what was going on. Clara singled out Mrs Braithwaite as the best gossip among them and stepped over to her. Quietly she whispered in her ear.

"Dear great uncle Ernest. Came down late last night, you might have seen the car that dropped him off. Lovely fellow, but too fond of his port. Though I suppose breathing your last at a family dinner with a decanter at your elbow is not such a bad way to go."

"He died at dinner?" Mrs Braithwaite gasped.

"Went face-down in his soup. Dreadful business. It was pea and mint."

"Oh you poor things!"

"He was eighty-five. We fully expected this to be his last visit, but not quite so literally." Clara gave a sigh, "I suppose I better finish that letter to his wife."

"Oh my, he was married? What will the poor love do now?"

"I expect she shall remarry."

"Really?"

"Well yes. She's only twenty-five." Clara left Mrs Braithwaite with that little golden nugget of fictitious gossip, content in the knowledge that her neighbours would now be too absorbed in discussing the moral vagaries of old men marrying young women to ever even consider that Clara had had a mummy in her house. In fact, before she had reached her front door several ladies had gathered around Mrs Braithwaite to hear what Clara had told her. Before teatime the story would have been so embellished and mismanaged that even if it had been the truth, there would be nothing of fact left in it.

Clara stepped into her hall and firmly closed the door behind her. Great uncles were very handy for these sorts of situations, far enough removed that no one was surprised they had never seen them before, yet close enough to suggest the family should be given a modicum of privacy while they overcame their grief. Clara went into the parlour and sat in the soft armchair by the fire. She pried off her shoes which were beginning to pinch and wriggled her stocking-clad toes with some satisfaction.

"Has Mervin Grimes made his exit?" Tommy rolled into the parlour.

"Yes. By the way I told the neighbours a great uncle had died."

"How dreadful."

"I know."

"I wish I could lie as easily as you Clara." Tommy gave his sister a mock serious look.

She put her tongue out at him.

"How did the doctor's appointment go?"

"He has hope he can help, so that at least makes one of us." Tommy shrugged.

"Don't be maudlin, I'm sure we will get you walking again."

Tommy didn't answer. His opinions on the subject were far less optimistic than his sister's. He decided to change the subject.

"While I was waiting at the doctor's I got talking to this woman who was planning on coming to see you. Her son went missing at the end of the war."

"Oh dear."

"Yes, I know, but this is an unusual case because he

was German and he was interned from 1914 on the Isle of Man. Anyway, the woman had hardly any money so I said not to worry about fees."

"Wait a moment," Clara held up a finger, "Weren't you the one who told me off for constantly taking on cases for free?"

"That's not the point…"

"Precisely is the point!"

"Anyway," Tommy said a little loudly to stop the argument, "I thought that as you were clearly busy with this Mervin Grimes business that I would take on the case of the lost German son, then it doesn't matter if it is done for free, as no one pays me anyway."

Clara was quiet a moment, a smile playing on her lips.

"That sounds a logical plan to me."

"Good. Well I've made a start. I rang up the Liverpool central train station to see if they have any records of this young man boarding a train there. He last told his mother he was heading home, you see."

"And if he didn't get on the train?"

Tommy opened his mouth before he realised he wasn't sure of the answer to that question.

"Perhaps you will need to contact the Liverpool police? I wonder if the army was involved in guarding the internment camp? Perhaps they kept records?"

"Yes, but he left the camp and was heading home a free man."

"It's all useful background information. In any case I doubt the army or police just waved off a load of German prisoners without keeping a quiet eye on them to make sure they headed back to the places they were supposed to. No, I would be very surprised if this young man did not board the train. At least up until that point he was probably watched. Afterwards anything could happen." Clara stretched one foot out and eased the tight muscles in her calf, "It's what I would do if I was in the authorities' footsteps. Keep a close watch until the prisoners were safely out of my jurisdiction. After that it is someone else's problem."

Tommy considered this.

"The train is my only lead. If he boarded it I know he was probably headed for London and I have a clue as to the next place he went. If not I don't know a thing."

"Try the Liverpool police, someone was keeping records on these men. If you find some people who knew your missing man they might be able to offer you clues."

"Maybe they would know why he vanished too. Thanks Clara."

"No problem." Clara smiled, "Just don't start usurping me as a private detective."

"Would I do that?"

"Once you have the use of your legs back there'll be no stopping you, I'll have competition."

Tommy made a snorting noise.

"I don't think you need worry about that."

"You are too negative Tommy, anything can happen."

"I think you and that Dr Cutt have more hope than sense." Tommy rolled his eyes.

His sister just gave him a sad smile, and he turned his head away. They both knew Tommy's hope had been squashed down into a tiny, tight little ball in the pit of his stomach, from where it rarely emerged.

"I'll just have to hope for both of us." Clara said softly.

Tommy didn't dare meet her eyes.

"You do that."

Chapter Ten

Clara was not expecting to meet Oliver Bankes in the police station, though admittedly, as a part-time police photographer, it was always possible he would be there. It was the day after Mervin Grimes had gone to the morgue and Clara had come to the police station to see if there was anything in their records concerning Mervin Grimes. Or rather, she had come to see if there was anything useful in their records, as she was confident they had an extensive library on the activities of the Black Hand gang. She was surprised to see Oliver in the entrance, not least because he tried to avoid her at first.

"Oliver?"

He looked embarrassed. In another person Clara might have called it 'shifty', but she preferred to be more generous with Oliver. She hoped nothing was wrong.

"Has there been a crime committed you must photograph?" She asked.

"Er, no. I'm not here on official business." Oliver shrugged his shoulders and avoided her eyes.

Clara found herself turning to the desk sergeant for insight into the strange behaviour of Oliver Bankes.

"Mr Bankes, they will be releasing your father from the cells shortly." The desk sergeant said helpfully, pushing a paper bag across his counter, "Here are your father's belongings and his camera. You may appreciate the used plates have been disposed of."

"Thank you." Oliver said through tight lips.

Now Clara was really curious.

"Oliver, what has happened? Is your father all right?"

"Just a misunderstanding." Oliver shrugged his shoulders.

"That's a funny way of saying he was taking inappropriate pictures." The desk sergeant was being far more helpful than usual and Clara decided that whatever had happened had quite amused him.

"What has he done, Oliver?" Clara insisted.

"Really, it is nothing!" Oliver hissed.

"He was caught red-handed photographing those nude birds at the fairground." The desk sergeant announced rather loudly with a grin.

Oliver looked mortified and Clara felt sorry for him.

"Perhaps, like Colonel Brandt, he misread the sign over the Exotic Birds' tent. It is rather misleading." She said, hoping her tact would rub off on the sergeant.

"No Clara, he knew exactly what he was doing." Oliver groaned, "He had already taken six plates before the fairground manager caught up with him. Some were apparently quite indecent."

"Oh." Clara was beginning to wish she had not skipped breakfast to get to the police station early. Had she indulged in some toast and honey, as Annie had wanted her to, then she would have missed Oliver's discomfort and spared him from the extra embarrassment.

"They're not charging him with anything, but he has been warned." Oliver continued forlornly, "I've got to try and keep an eye on him."

"Parents can be such a chore." Clara sympathised.

"You won't mention this to anyone?" Oliver asked desperately.

Clara touched his arm.

"I am good with secrets."

Thanks. Look, here comes the old sot now."

Mr Bankes emerged from the back of the station looking sheepish.

"I see you have my camera safe Oliver." He smiled at his son and politely nodded to Clara, "Good morning Miss Fitzgerald, I've had a little bit of bother. Nothing to worry about, complete misunderstanding."

The desk sergeant gave a strangled snort which suggested he was trying to suppress a s+nigger. Clara threw him a meaningful look.

"Let's just get home father." Oliver grabbed up the paper bag and camera, "Clara's got things to do."

"Nice seeing you again Miss Fitzgerald, come around for tea one Sunday." Mr Bankes gave Clara another nod then followed his son out of the station.

"Watch out for that one." The desk sergeant said in a low voice, tilting his head in the direction of Mr Bankes, "I know his type. No matter what your friend said, his old man knew exactly what he was about. Never have trusted these photographer-types, they like gawping at people too much."

"I'll bear that in mind." Clara assured him before she headed around the desk and down a long corridor towards the archive room.

Mr Bankes' indiscretion was rapidly forgotten as she strolled through the stacks of shelves and found a large section devoted to criminal gangs, among them a hefty file on the Black Hand. She set it on a table and opened the front page.

"The Black Hand, now I recall, that was the name of the rebel group who orchestrated the assassination of Archduke Franz Ferdinand." Clara said to herself, "Somehow I doubt you were part of that Mr Grimes."

She flicked over a couple of pages featuring names, descriptions and mug-shots of known gang members. Most looked like youths who had known little else in life but crime. A couple were older, but the average age of a Black Hand member was definitely under thirty. It struck Clara that these were not experienced criminals and the lists of arrest charges confirmed that idea. Most of the gang were pickpockets, with the odd violent assault charge thrown in for good measure. Things only got interesting when she reached Mervin Grimes.

Mervin wanted more than a life of petty disorder. If he was going to be a criminal he was going to at least make it worth his while. A prison sentence at sixteen for petty theft had clearly not sat well with him, after that he aimed for bigger things. Mervin found his way into organised rings of race fixers, while doing a bit of pimping on the side. While the rest of the gang amused themselves with run-of-the-mill street crime, Mervin was making a name for himself. He helped fix a race when he was seventeen and was caught soon after. Charged for doping a horse, he went down for a few months, but was soon back out. He had learned from his mistake. There were no further arrests for Mervin, though the police were clearly suspicious of him and knew he was running with some dangerous crowds.

He was implicated in five more race fixing scandals, each one scooping more money than the last. But it was his final fix, the one before he disappeared, that took the biscuit. Mervin and his pals not only ensured a 200 to 1 odds horse finished first, but they screwed over a rival gang of race fixers who were down from London. The local boys had scored against the outsiders, but it was very much an own goal. Criminals who lose a lot of money don't tend to leave the scene quietly. In fact a spate of vicious murders shortly after the race indicated how displeased their London rivals were. Mervin's disappearance was treated as just another of these revenge killings.

In all honesty Clara could see the police's logic and was almost prepared to accept the obvious. Almost. Because all the other victims had been found. That had been the point. Take Billy 'Razor' Brown, for instance. He was found under Brighton pier, his fingers smashed, his throat slit and his pockets still full of his share of the winnings. It was plain to see this was a warning to other rivals who thought they could best the City boys. All the murders had followed similar patterns; a few had even been drawn to the police's attention by anonymous tips that suggested the Londoners were making doubly sure their messages were found. Mervin, however, just vanished.

Of course, one should never rule out the obvious. For all Clara knew Mervin was meant to be found, but fate took a hand and his body ended up concealed. He was shot, after all, and several of the other victims had perished that way too. Trouble was, Clara couldn't see how she could trace London mob boys, at least not safely. She returned to the shelves and found there were a few files on the thugs from London, clearly the Brighton police were keeping tabs of trouble-makers on their holidays. She cross-checked the suspect names in the Black Hand killings against these files and came up with a pile of five. All but one were still apparently alive, but that didn't help much. Clara scribbled down their names, but felt herself rapidly running into a dead end. It was time, she decided, to look at things from the other direction. Mervin's corpse had been on quite a journey, if she could narrow down how he ended up in a fairground masquerading as a pharaoh, just maybe she would have a clue to his killer.

She returned the files and gathered up her hat and bag, a new purpose in her actions. One way or the other she would fathom out the last chapter in Mervin's life. She just hoped it wouldn't be one that led her into dangerous company.

The fair was due to be around until the end of the month, so the stall-holders, ride operators and performers had settled into their surroundings, 10 o'clock in the morning was a little early for much trade, aside from some mothers with small children. Things would liven up as the afternoon drifted into evening, for the moment things were almost peaceful and several of the fairground residents were taking the opportunity to relax for a while. Clara walked past the Siamese twins eating popcorn from a paper bag and arguing in a foreign tongue. A little further on she spotted the prim mermaid, now tail-less, flirting with the fair's strongman. It seemed everyone had emerged from their dark tents and caravans to make the most of the sunshine. Except Bowmen. Clara wondered if the man ever ventured into daylight or, like Dracula in that horrid film Tommy had insisted on taking his sister to see, he cowered back at the burning rays of sunshine. Clara knocked on the door of his caravan. There was no response.

"Derek doesn't like entertaining people at this time of day."

Clara turned and found herself before the now non-bearded lady, Jane Porter.

"I really must speak to him." Clara said.

"Is it about Hepkaptut?"

"Yes."

"There was trouble again last night." Jane pursed her lips, "Some fellows said they had come for the mummy and were not pleased when Derek told them he was gone."

"What did these fellows want?"

"They didn't say, but something was itching in their britches. I thought they were going to try and hit Derek, and that would have been a bad move. Aside from the many 'helpers' Derek employs for the purposes of sorting out trouble, he is a dab hand with a right hook himself."

"You know Mr Bowmen well?"

"Rather! He was the one that discovered me, if that's the word for it." Jane gave a sad sigh, "It's not a happy thing being a girl who has to shave every morning. Derek brought his travelling show through my old village one day. It wasn't as grand as all this then, of course. At the time I had taken to going around wearing a veil, but everyone knew about my problem, that's the sort of secret village folk love to share. In any case, Derek heard about me and he made me an offer. I could live all my life beneath a veil or join his show and display my abnormality. To be honest I didn't really see there was much choice."

"It must be hard travelling all the time."

"Not really. You get used to it and these days I have my own caravan. Though, as bearded ladies go, I am not much of a specimen at the moment."

"I don't know, I'm sure I see a bit of stubble on your chin." Clara said helpfully.

"Thank you." Jane smiled, "I never thought I would miss it so."

"Look, perhaps you can help me? Does Mr Bowmen keep records for the fair?"

"Naturally."

"So he could tell me when Hepkaptut became one of the exhibits?"

"Oh, even I can tell you that. It was about a year ago."

"Where did he come from?"

"That I can't say, look, come for a cup of coffee and I shall try and answer your questions. By the time we are done Derek might have roused himself."

Jane Porter led the way through the tents to a small stand with a big hot water urn and a man dressed in a turban. The decoration around the stall and the name above proclaimed he was selling the best Turkish coffee ever found in England.

"Two cups, Fred." Jane asked the man who responded with 'righto' in a Scottish accent.

Jane motioned to several deckchairs in front of the stall, picking out one for herself and waiting for Clara to sit in the next one, before she carried on talking.

"The war really made life hard for us." Jane explained, "A lot of the young fellows joined up, of course, can't blame them. And we had several of our steam engines requisitioned for the war effort. What was left over was us ladies, and the odds and sods too old for war, or too different. We fended for ourselves as best we could. Derek managed to wrangle his way out of serving, I never asked how. We travelled with a smaller fair, but it wasn't easy. Derek came up with the idea of making it a patriotic affair, lots of flags and pictures of the king, and donating so much of our takings to the war effort. That helped, but lots of people just couldn't bring themselves to enjoy the fair when far away their men were dying. In any case, by 1916 travelling was too difficult. Our last horses had been spirited away into the British army, so there was no one to pull our wagons. Derek rented a small field for the caravans, threw tarpaulins over the remaining rides, and told us to sit tight and hope. I did a shift in a munitions factory for a time. That was quite amusing."

The look on Jane' face as she remembered this implied it had been quite the opposite. The Scottish man in the turban brought over their coffees and Clara peered into the deep depths of the sultry brown drink. She was not a fan of coffee, especially black.

"For two years you just kicked your heels?" Clara asked, stirring her spoon suspiciously in the dark liquid.

"Pretty much. Us show folk are not much good at saving money, so it was a bad time. Armless Arnold nearly starved to death."

"When did you begin to tour again?"

"December 1918! Don't think us callous, but we needed the work. As soon as the victory bells had stopped ringing off we went. Took some doing finding new steam engines and horses, and rounding up performers and rides, not to mention helpers. But we got there and ever since then Derek has been making the fair bigger and better."

"Which is why he bought Hepkaptut?"

Jane took a long sip of her coffee, clearly enjoying the bitter taste as it slipped down her throat.

"Hepkaptut is part of the sideshows, every fair needs them. For times of the day like this when no one is performing but people want to see things. And they are cheap. They don't eat or need paying, and they bring in the public. Curiosities, novelties, sometimes downright frauds, they are all part and parcel of the fair."

"Where do these novelties generally come from?" Clara risked a sip of her drink, trying not to pull a face as she drank.

"Derek has contacts who deal in those sorts of things." Jane shrugged, "I suppose they find them in house clearances and junk shops. I know the two-headed calf came from Scotland where it had been stuffed and mounted for a Lord of the manor who thought himself an amateur naturalist."

"But you don't know where Hepkaptut came from?"

"I know it was one of Derek's dealer friends. We were in Cornwall passing those dull days between Christmas and Easter when no one can be bothered with fairs. This dealer stops by any time we are passing through the area and offers Derek a first look at any new merchandise. I believe he supplies a number of fairground operators." Jane took more coffee, "He had brought over a shrunken head, said to be that of a missionary who went to Fiji, and a stuffed tiger which he claimed had tried to kill a member of the royal family before being shot by a valiant native in India. Quite frankly they were dull things, no wonder the mummy caught Derek's attention."

"Did the mummy have a story too?"

"Something about it being unearthed in Egypt a century ago. A lost king that no one knew existed. Said it had been in private hands, until it reached him. That's about all I remember. It gave me the creeps then and it still does now."

"And you can't remember the name of this man?"

"No. Derek will have the details. Look, don't judge us too harshly. Everyone knows the fair is nothing but illusion. Hepkaptut might not have been Egyptian, but he looked the part and Derek was thinking about paying the bills."

"I don't blame any of you, I am just trying to discover how a murdered man ended up on display in the House of

Curios."

"Murdered?"

"The living Hepkaptut was alive and well fifteen years ago in Brighton, then he vanished. All these years later he turns up at a fairground. Here, you are looking a little shocked, have my coffee."

Clara handed over the foul drink and Jane drank it almost in one.

"That's awful!"

"Do you think Mr Bowmen will be able to speak to me now?"

"Even if he isn't I'll wake him!" Jane said firmly, hoisting herself up from her deck chair, "And to think I had that... that... corpse in my caravan!"

She led the way back to Bowmen's caravan and personally hammered on the door to gain attention.

"Derek? Are you in? Someone needs to speak to you!"

There was a muffled voice from within and a thud that sounded like a shoe being thrown at the door.

"I'm not leaving until you let me in." Jane said without reacting to the sound, "Do you hear me?"

A second thud suggested the shoe's pair had also been thrown.

"He is really bad in the mornings." Jane spoke conspiratorially over her shoulder to Clara, then went back to hollering at the door, "Come on Derek, it's nearly midday!"

Finally the door swung open and a dishevelled Derek Bowmen, wearing a crumpled shirt and a bleary expression, glowered at them.

"Wha..?"

"This lady needs to speak to you." Jane pointed out Clara.

A nasty look crept onto Bowmen's face, it was the sort of look a man might give a rat that has just crawled over his foot and stolen his last slice of bread. Clara felt distinctly uncomfortable.

"I loaned you the mummy, what more you want?"

"I have a few questions." Stated Clara, "It won't take long if you have your records book to hand."

Bowmen was not impressed.

"You know how much trouble you have caused me? Why is everyone looking for that damn mummy?"

"I'm not entirely certain," Clara admitted, "Which is why I thought you could help me. I need to know who sold you Hepkaptut."

"Donovan Ruskin, dealer in Cornwall." Bowmen snorted, "Satisfied?"

He was about to close his door, but Jane wedged her foot firmly in it.

"Did he say where he had come by it?" Clara asked.

"No, and I didn't care. Look, he said it was an ancient mummy. I'm not exactly an expert on those sorts of things, so if it was wrong it was wrong. I thought he looked the part with the headdress and all."

"Do you have an address for Donovan Ruskin?"

Grumbling, Bowmen vanished into his caravan and returned a moment latter with a card that read 'Ruskin Antiques, House Clearance, Furniture Removal, Free Evaluations'.

"Is that it?"

"For the moment." Clara said coolly, "Hepkaptut has been identified as a man who died fifteen years ago."

"So?"

"He was murdered Mr Bowmen."

Derek Bowmen didn't even blink.

"Guess I'll have to find another pharaoh then." He snatched his door and gave Jane a small shove so he could slam it shut in their faces.

"He can be a sweetie when he wants to." Jane apologised to Clara.

"Who could I ask about the men who have been causing a bother around here?" Clara had decided Bowmen was a dead loss.

"Black Pete's in charge of security. I can show you to his caravan, he is probably there at this time of day.

Unlike Derek he is on duty the entire time the fair is open."

Jane led Clara back through the fairground and towards the far side where most of the acts had their accommodation. Several sleepy-eyed performers were just rousing themselves from their slumbers and starting half-hearted practice routines. Clara noted some Chinese acrobats tumbling in a corner and a juggler who couldn't stop yawning as he threw balls in the air.

"We are night folk." Jane said, stepping daintily over a pile of horse manure dropped by an Arabian with a white feather topping its head, "Most of us only perform after 3pm and then on into the wee hours. It's a strange life, I suppose."

Jane took them to a caravan with a bull terrier sleeping outside. The dog raised its head and stared at them curiously.

"Take no notice of Punch." Jane patted the dog's head, "He is for appearances only. He is too soft to even chase a cat."

Though this was probably true, Clara felt it prudent to give the dog a wide berth. Punch lost interest and dropped back into a doze.

"Black Pete, are you in?" Jane hammered on Pete's door, she was good at hammering and the noise reverberated around the nearby caravans causing several people to look over curiously. Punch, however, feigned sleep.

The door on the caravan opened and though Clara half-expected to see an angry-faced man like Bowmen, Black Pete was apparently not concerned at being roused by vigorous knocking. He also failed to live up to his name. There was nothing very black about Pete, his hair was grey and his skin as pale as marble. Clara wondered how he had received a nickname so at odds with his appearance.

"What's the matter Jane?"

"This lady needs to speak with you, it's quite urgent."

Black Pete turned his attention on Clara.

"Is it a lost handbag? Or perhaps a child gone astray, the little ones get very distracted at the fair."

"It's nothing like that." Clara promised, wondering if she gave the appearance of a fraught mother seeking a lost child, "Actually I am here about the problems you have been having with Hepkaptut."

"For a dead fella he is certainly a nuisance." Black Pete agreed, "Would you ladies like to come into the old office."

The hospitality of Black Pete was certainly a far cry from that of Bowmen. He found Jane and Clara chairs and offered them tea and a biscuit, both politely refused, before settling himself in a decaying armchair that groaned unhappily as he sat down.

"So ladies, what is this all about?"

"My name is Clara Fitzgerald," Clara began, "I work as a private detective and I have been asked to investigate the death of Mervin Grimes, or King Hepkaptut as you know him, by his family."

"Gosh, so Hepkaptut was a real fella?" Pete felt a shiver of repulsion go down his spine, "Doesn't that make you think? All this time I thought he was some dummy made of paste and plaster. Never expected him to be a real man. I've seen some things during my time here, but that takes it all."

Black Pete was a man who took things at face value, a man who lived simply and didn't worry about difficult questions. That had served him well over the decade he had been a security man, but occasionally things cropped up that temporarily buffeted his simple thinking into dangerous territories of contemplation. Right now Black Pete's mind was going over the times he had handled King Hepkaptut without a concern and it was giving him the creeps. He helped himself to three biscuits to settle his nerves.

"The thing is Mr…" Clara faltered before recovering herself, "Pete, the thing is, Mervin Grimes' body has been drawing a lot of attention since it arrived back in Brighton. Perhaps you can tell me more about that."

Black Pete stopped munching his third Garibaldi.

"You want to know about the break-in the other night I suppose?"

Clara nodded.

"Well they didn't get very far, smashed the glass on Hepkaptut's… I mean, Mr Grimes' case, but there was too many people around and someone raised the alarm. I found them trying to prise his arm off, of all things."

"Really?"

"I presume that is what they were doing. Anyway they were yanking at his arm and screaming at each other. I went in with three of my best lads and they legged it as fast as they could."

"What did these men look like?"

Black Pete had to take a moment to circle his thoughts back to that evening. He wasn't usually called upon to remember much.

"Three of 'em. Wearing what I would call Sunday suits. Dressed up for the fair, I imagine. Not so young either, at least one was my age. One was just a lad, the other was a grown man. Worker types. Rough hands, faces full of cares. Probably only had a few pence in their pockets and were hoping to make a night of it at someone else's expense."

"You think they were opportunists?"

"I did at the time. You see King Hepkaptut, when he is dressed in his finery, looks quite swanky. But it's all paste and glass, nothing of value, any fool would realise that, at least you would think."

Clara nodded again, making no mention that at least one object on Hepkaptut was of potential value. That ring on his finger would be attractive to any thief but, more importantly, it could tell any surviving member of the Black Hand just who was in the case, as it had Oliver. Supposing someone realised a murder victim was on display at the fair and was worried someone else might find out?

"Since that night have these three men returned."

"Probably." Black Pete shrugged, "I glimpsed them, that's all. Even if I gave my lads a description of the three, finding them among the hundreds of people in here at any one time would be virtually impossible. If they wanted to come back, and they had the sense to do so at a busy time, I doubt anyone would notice."

"So there has been no specific further trouble?"

"Do you mean that business at Bowmen's caravan? Someone tried to steal the master keys. He has a spare for every caravan, stall and money box, just in case. But they are always locked in a safe in his caravan. They got as far as opening a window before someone noticed. My lads were on it in a flash, but they legged it. To be honest most of my job is just chasing people away. I couldn't say for certain they were the same fellows who were after Hepkaptut."

"If you ask me that mummy was trouble the moment it came here." Jane Porter suddenly piped up, "They talk about pharaoh's curses, and I think that had one."

"But the mummy isn't ancient Egyptian." Clara protested.

"Doesn't matter, there was something wrong about that mummy. It gave me goosebumps every time I saw it." Jane touched her bare chin sadly, "I swear our takings have been down since it arrived."

Black Pete gave a shake of his head, as if such a thought was beyond him. Very possibly it was, Pete would be the first to admit he had no imagination.

"Well thank you very much for explaining that." Clara decided it was time to take her leave.

"It was really no bother." Black Pete answered, ushering the ladies to his door, "I suppose I ought to do my rounds."

He followed Clara and Jane outside and stretched in the fresh air.

"Come on Punch, let's see what's what. Good day

ladies." Pete gave them another nod and wandered off with the bull terrier following his heels.

"Thank you Jane, I can see myself out." Clara turned to her guide.

"If you need anything else, just ask." Jane answered amiably.

"Perhaps you could keep an ear out for any gossip concerning Mervin Grimes?" Clara held out one of her cards, "You can contact me here."

"All right, I'll keep my ears pinned back. Nothing better to do after all." Jane grinned, "One word of advice thought, take care how you go."

Clara rolled her eyes as she turned to leave.

"As I tell everyone else, I always do."

Chapter Eleven

Tommy had followed Clara's advice and contacted the Liverpool police division who had ultimately passed him on to an office that dealt with railway offences, who then transferred him to a bobby called PC William, who explained over the phone that he had been in charge of walking the beat past the central railway station for the last four years. Tommy felt he had been passed from pillar to post without getting any further, but when he raised the question of German internees William assured him that he was the right man to ask.

"I know all about the Sausage-eaters." He said loftily, "Was my job to keep an eye when they boarded them trains and set off for home. Has one of 'em committed a crime? You ask me they should all have been shot on sight. You can't trust a German."

A picture flashed through Tommy's mind of the grief-stricken Mrs Smith and her assurances that her son was as British as any native of the isle.

"I am trying to find a particular man who may have boarded the train and then vanished."

"Good riddance."

Tommy was surprised at how offensive he found this remark. A day ago he may not have exactly agreed with it, but certainly would have understood its sentiment.

Now he was wrapped up in thoughts of a grieving mother who had been through Hell and back just because she had the wrong accent. That made Tommy deeply uncomfortable.

"His name was Jurgen Smith, he was in his twenties, dark-haired."

PC William was silent on the phone, presumably thinking over the matter.

"Hello?"

"I was looking in my notebook. I kept a list of all the Germans who left at the end of 1918, just in case one proved to be a spy. I figured if I kept a record that would set me in a good light as someone who thinks ahead. Initiative, you see. I spoke to 'em all, though some insisted in speaking in that funny lingo of theirs. Drove me insane."

The phone clunked a little and William's voice seemed further away.

"I wrote down three Jurgen Smiths, they all call themselves the same thing, you know, no imagination."

Tommy was silent.

"Anyway," William rustled some paper, "I think the one you want was Jurgen Smith no.2. Left Liverpool on the 2.15, Thursday 12 December. He said he was heading to London."

"He definitely got on the train?" Tommy pressed.

"I made a note that he did so. I watched them all get on their trains just to be sure. I'm a thorough man Mr Fitzgerald."

"That you are PC William."

"Anything else I can do to help you?"

Tommy started to say no, then stopped himself. A thought had sprung to his mind.

"I don't suppose you know who Jurgen boarded the train with? The people who shared his compartment, I mean."

Tommy could hear paper rustling again. PC William struck him as a man who rarely used the phone and didn't understand that Tommy could not see him doing these things and that lengthy silences made one thing the connection had been lost.

"I wrote down two other Germans who got in the same carriage as Smith." William said after a long pause, "Alphonse Dieter and Hans Friger."

Tommy scribbled down the names, just maybe, he theorised, these were men who had been friendly with Jurgen. They might have all decided to share a carriage as they made their way home and even if they got into the same carriage by coincidence, they could be witnesses to what happened next.

"Do you have addresses for these men?" Tommy asked.

"Hang on. No.2 Green Drive, Guildford, Surrey for Dieter. Flat 3, Park House, Norwich, Norfolk for Friger. Does that help?"

"Thank you, yes, it helps a lot."

Tommy put down the phone and wondered if these were dead ends or leads? He was still waiting for the information from the Liverpool Stationmaster which might hold more clues, and there was one other source he could chase. Tommy went to his bedroom and searched in a drawer for a small, black diary. He didn't get the thing out often; probably it was over a year since he last looked at it. His reasons for keeping it were complicated and didn't entirely make sense even to himself, but his reasons for avoiding looking at it were quite simple; it was stained with blood, his blood. Some of the pages were stuck together and quite frankly it made him grimace just to hold it. The diary had been in his pocket on the day he was shot. It still even smelt of Flanders. Normally Tommy kept the diary hidden, not quite prepared to discard it. But today he needed something from it and he was prepared to brave the sickening feeling it gave him to touch the cover (and the nightmares that would no doubt follow) to extract a certain piece of information from it.

He flipped to the pages at the back of the book where

he had stored useful information. Names of the dead flashed in front of his eyes; at first he had crossed out their names and addresses when they had gone to meet their Maker, but that had become too demoralising an activity, so he had just started to ignore them. Now names flicked before his eyes and stirred that familiar, painful gripe of loss in his stomach. A knot that burned and twisted and threatened to make him gag. Percy, Frank, Stephen, John, all men he had known well and who had perished in that Hell of mud and shells. Morris, Ernest, Joshua, Sebastian. Gassed, shelled, buried alive, died of flu.

Tommy shut the book and got a grip on himself. Old names, old friends. He had to let it go. He opened the pages again and tried not to read every entry. Why had he written so many down? Back then he had diligently recorded these addresses in the naive certainty that one day he would write to these same people, when the war was long over and they were old men who wanted to reminisce about their youth. Even when they all started dying he somehow couldn't stop. His diary had become a list of the dead.

He turned another page, fingers shaking, and there was the one he wanted. Edward Beard. He wrote down the address on a fresh piece of paper as fast as he could. Captain Edward Beard had been his superior, now he was a brigadier. Once, on some dark, God forsaken night Tommy hardly remembered, he had saved the life of Captain Edward Beard. Pulling him half-conscious out of a shell hole just as another round pounded down nearby. Beard had assured Tommy he would be eternally grateful and would return the favour whenever he could. Tommy was cynical about such oaths said in the heat of battle, but just perhaps Beard had meant it, and if he had now was the prime opportunity to call in a favour. After all, who better than a brigadier to find out what military records had been kept concerning the internees on the Isle of Man?

Tommy dialled the number for Beard's brigade headquarters, hoping they would know how to get in touch with him.

Brigadier Edward Beard in general did not receive calls from people he knew in the trenches, in fact he didn't receive phone calls from civilians at all. That, he felt, was what secretaries were for. But when Mrs Burrows came in looking a little ragged and explaining that the man on the other end of the line was very insistent and refused to hang up, it gave Beard pause for thought.

"What is his name?" The aging soldier asked.

"He says he is Private Thomas Fitzgerald."

Beard gave this due consideration, not, he would have people understand, because he could not remember one Thomas Fitzgerald. For the actions of that brave man were forever etched in his mind. Rather because Brigadier Beard always gave everything due consideration, he found that this was the best means of avoiding embarrassing decisions.

"Put him through to me." He said after a good minute had elapsed.

Tommy found the familiar voice that suddenly came on the line rather disconcerting. It brought back memories of a time he dearly wanted to forget.

"Private Fitzgerald."

"Brigadier Beard, Sir. Congratulations on your promotion, Sir."

Even after two years as a civilian it came naturally to Tommy to revert to strict military protocol, somehow there seemed no other way of addressing Beard.

"Thank you Fitzgerald. I assume you are calling in that favour I owe you?"

Tommy had to smile to himself. Beard had not changed.

"Yes Sir."

"If you want me to open some fete or gala day, I really am rather busy. I know there isn't a war on, but I still have work to do."

"I'm afraid it's something a bit more delicate than that, Sir."

"Really?" Beard paused, giving this latest information its due consideration, "Perhaps you better explain Fitzgerald."

"Well Sir, I am looking into the disappearance of a young man, only it is slightly awkward because he was a German internee."

"How did you get mixed up with that?"

"His mother presented the case to me, Sir."

"Lots of British mothers lost sons in the war and don't know what happened to them."

"I appreciate that, Sir. But this man went missing on English soil and that makes me concerned. After all, he was a civilian who had lived in London since he was an infant."

Beard mused again.

"What have you done so far?"

"Gathered information from the police and station authorities in Liverpool. I'm still waiting on the latter, but the police say he was released from internment on the Isle of Man and then boarded a train at Liverpool. Somewhere after that he vanished. I was hoping you might be able to help me learn more details about his time at the internment camp and also about two men who boarded the same carriage as him."

Beard whistled through his teeth.

"You are asking me to look into private files."

"Yes, Sir, but only because I need something to help me track this man. Perhaps there was something in his history on the Isle of Man that could give me clues as to what happened. I don't expect to find this man alive, you understand."

"They are still classified files." Beard tutted.

"I know Sir."

There was a long silence. Beard stared at the wooden door in his office and his mind drifted back four years.

"His name was Jurgen Smith, Sir." Tommy decided to give his superior officer a nudge.

"Anything could have happened to him. Lots of anti-German sentiment when the war ended." Beard muttered noncommittally.

"Yes, Sir, but Jurgen had a London accent. No one would have suspected him of being a German unless he told them, and that is unlikely. I rather imagine he was either the victim of an accident or was accosted by someone he knew. Hence I have a couple of names it would be useful to have background information on."

"Fitzgerald, you are asking an awful lot."

"I know, Sir."

Beard sighed.

"How have you been since the war?" He asked, it was a leading question.

"Not too bad, Sir. Lost the use of my legs in 1917, though."

"That's a shame." Beard paused, "I still remember that night. Because of you I lived to become a brigadier."

"Yes, Sir."

"Not everyone would have risked themselves like that. I have always felt myself in debt to you for my life."

Tommy gave no reply. Beard tapped his fingers on his desk.

"It isn't unheard of for a senior officer to want to look in classified files." Beard spoke to himself, but naturally Tommy could hear him, "You couldn't use the information in a court of law, if this fellow has been murdered, I mean."

"Obviously, Sir."

"But it would be possible. I would be putting my neck on the line for you, but it would certainly be safer than clambering into a shell crater in the middle of a bombardment. I didn't survive the war to become a deskbound coward afraid to take a risk or two."

"No, Sir."

"But this would be the one and only time Fitzgerald."

"I completely understand Sir."

Beard gave another long sigh, his mind made up.

"Give me those names then Fitzgerald, and I shall see what I can do. I have a friend in the Home Office, might be able to help me get access."

"Thank you, Sir." Tommy read out the three names and then gave Beard his address, "This is much appreciated, Sir."

"No doubt. Take care of yourself Fitzgerald."

"Will do, Sir." Tommy barely finished speaking and the line went dead. He returned the receiver to its holder and then felt as though he had been mentally shaken from head to foot. Hearing the deep, booming sound of Beard's voice brought back a thousand memories of mud, blood and dead men. The last hour had been rather an ordeal for Tommy and he was feeling rather sick. He closed his eyes and tried to steady his nerves. He was going to pay for all this digging up the past with nightmares in the wee hours. He just knew it.

Chapter Twelve

Clara had bought herself an ice cream. It wasn't exactly ice cream weather, as a thick bank of grey cloud was gathering over Brighton and threatening heavy rain. But she had felt like something sweet and the ice cream man had been standing just at the gates of the fairground as she left. She had lied to herself and declared that ice cream was much healthier for her than any of the alternatives on offer, such as hot American doughnuts.

She had walked into Brighton high street pondering over her latest findings and her footsteps had led her to Oliver's photography shop. In her mind was the idea that she should pop in and console Oliver over the morning's events, after all he need not be embarrassed as he had personally done nothing wrong. Unfortunately, when she pushed on the door she found it locked. This was unusual. Oliver had many flaws, including being completely disorganised and untidy, but he was very good at running his shop and he never closed during working hours unless he had been called out by the police. And when that happened, he always put a sign in the door explaining he was on police business. Today the only sign present was one that read 'closed'.

Clara licked her ice cream thoughtfully. Oliver lived in a flat above his shop, but there was no bell for his private residence. Oliver rarely entertained and did not expect callers outside office hours. Since his shop was often open until late in the evening to accommodate customers who worked during the day, Clara understood why Oliver would feel it necessary to be able to retire to his flat and ignore the world. If he was in his flat there was no easy way to contact him.

Clara pulled a notebook from her handbag and quickly wrote out a note explaining that he need not be concerned on her behalf about the events of that morning and that she had some interesting new information on the case if he was interested. She popped the note through the letterbox as another idea dawned on her. There was one other place he might be.

Clara found her way easily enough to the residence of Mr Bankes. There was no evidence of trouble at the property, so she knocked on the door. Oliver answered with a scowl on his face.

"Clara?" His expression changed to wide-eyed surprise.

"Your shop is shut." Clara said simply.

"Well... yes. It's been a rather challenging day."

"Is your father well?"

"Don't talk about him!" Oliver's scowl returned and he abruptly stepped out of the house and shut the door behind him, "I was about to head home anyway."

Oliver started to storm up the path and Clara followed him after momentarily casting her gaze back at the house.

"He doesn't see he did anything wrong." Oliver said, his anger palpable, "They could have charged him with making indecent images!"

"But they didn't." Clara said gently, taking Oliver's arm.

"I just don't trust him to behave himself."

"He's an old man, I doubt he can get into too much trouble as long as we keep him away from fairgrounds."

"In any case, I'm sorry you witnessed this morning."

"Oh tosh! I've witnessed a lot worse." Clara laughed,

"Now let's go open your shop, I want to take another look at those photos you have of Mervin Grimes. Oh, but first I want to invite someone to join us, if you don't mind."

"As long as it isn't my father." Oliver mumbled.

An hour later Bob Waters was sitting at Oliver's shop counter going over the last photographs ever taken of Mervin Grimes.

"Don't he look dapper?" Bob said sadly, "I always wanted a bowler hat like that."

"Tell me Bob, do you remember anything special Mervin might have said about that ring he is wearing."

Bob drew an imaginary circle around Mervin's black and white hand with a large finger.

"It had an initial in it that didn't mean anything as far as I could make out. But I suppose it could have been for something he hadn't told me about. He was like that in the end. Secretive."

"He had had the ring a long time?"

"Since he was sixteen. Came home wearing it one day, was dead proud of it, but wouldn't say why or how he had got it. Do you think it was valuable?"

"I'm not sure. Bob, have you any idea what Mervin did with his last big winnings?"

"Aside from spending it?"

"Yes, aside from that."

Bob studied the photo of his old friend.

"I don't know, wish I did because his old mum could use it. She needs the pipes doing and the chimney repairing, not to mention the upstairs windows. Oh, I do some of it, but there is only so much I can do for free."

"I understand that." Clara said, "Does Mrs Grimes have no other family?"

"Just Mervin. He was her all. Broke her heart when he vanished. She sat in her window for over a year waiting for him to come back, convinced he had just gone up to London all of a sudden."

Oliver came over with a cup of tea for Mervin and Clara. He pulled a picture of Mervin towards himself and looked at it for a long while.

"I have some names of people Mervin might have known," Clara continued, "I wondered if you could tell me anything about them?"

"I'll try." Bob promised.

"Right, what about Richard 'Dixie' Doncaster?"

Bob scrunched his face into a squashed ball of concentration then shook his head.

"Patrick MacKillip?"

Another shake.

"Felix 'Beggar' Mundell?"

Bob closed his eyes, thought for a moment, then gave another negative.

"Penny Palmer?"

"Oh wait, I know that one. She was a girl he brought home once. Mrs Grimes hated her, said she thought herself too good for what she was. Penny went out with Mervin for about a year."

"Was she part of the Black Hand?"

Bob shrugged.

"Maybe, if she was with Mervin he might have introduced her to the gang." Bob scratched at his thick, curling head of hair, "She was a pretty one, if you like 'em skinny. But she had this touch of nastiness to her. She was quiet, sullen even, until you wronged her and then this spiteful hussy emerged. And it didn't take much to get on her bad side. Say the wrong word, or forget sugar for her tea and she would lose it. I never knew what to say to her. She scared the living daylights out of me."

"Where did she live?"

"Margate, at least that's where her folks where. I think she stayed with friends a lot."

"Was she with Mervin when he disappeared?"

"Let me think." Bob concentrated hard again, running through some mental calendar unique to himself, "Yes, I reckon so. Because Mrs Grimes kept saying if he had run off with that hussy she would never speak to him again."

Clara drew a star next to Penny Palmer's name in her

notebook, definitely a line of inquiry to follow up.

"Can you think of any other friends of Mervin's that I should speak too?"

Bob was clearly finding all this concentrated thinking a tough business. He gulped down his tea and then scratched at his head again, his brow creasing into furrows as he dug around in his brain for memories.

"You could talk to Mickey Walker. I think he sometimes helped the Black Hand. He's a plumber by trade, but working for a living never suited him." Bob grinned, "I can't think of no one else, sorry."

"You have been more than useful Bob, I appreciate you coming here." Clara smiled, "Out of all of his friends you were clearly the most loyal."

Bob shifted in his seat uncomfortably.

"I don't know about that, I just tried to help Mervin and for his sake his mum. Not that she lets me help much. I was going to give Mervin's room a lick of paint, make it all fresh for if he ever returned. She would have none of it. 'You leave my Mervin's things alone.' She yelled at me."

"Perhaps she felt if you decorated, it would be removing her last connection to Mervin?" Clara suggested.

"I guess." Bob looked suddenly very sad, "I thought I was helping. I know I ain't the brightest of things, and the boxing didn't exactly make me brighter, but I do try for folk. Mrs Grimes does seem to shout at me a lot."

"Never mind Bob." Clara patted his hand comfortingly, "Sometimes when we are grieving it is easiest to take it out on the people we care about the most."

"Really?"

"Sometimes."

Bob mused on this.

"I don't think Mrs Grimes cares for me, I know you are trying to be kind, but I really don't think she gives a damn about me." Bob grinned, "It was jolly nice of you giving me a cup of tea, but might I go now? I have a window to fix and a Welsh dresser to varnish."

"Of course Bob. Thank you for coming."

Bob gave another grin, rose from his chair (which groaned in relief at the removal of his weight) and wandered out into the August drizzle.

"Nice fellow, can't see what he wanted to be doing with Mervin Grimes." Oliver said, giving the photo of the gangster a scowl.

"No, I suppose it is one of those things." Clara answered, "My word, is that the time? Where has the day gone?"

Clara stood and started collecting up her handbag when she paused. A thought had struck her.

"Come to dinner Oliver." She said spontaneously.

Oliver gave a wry smile.

"Off that table Mervin Grimes lay on?"

"It's perfectly clean." Clara pretended to be offended, "In any case, I don't want you moping about in your flat, so come to dinner."

"I don't mope."

"You do. You are very maudlin at the moment."

Oliver pulled a face.

"It's the weather." He nodded out the window at the rain.

"Come to dinner and take your mind off things." Clara insisted.

Oliver made one last pretence at reluctance than gave in. He grabbed his own hat and an umbrella from a stand by the door before they left the shop.

"Mervin's ring is playing on my mind." Clara said as he locked the door.

"Why?"

"There's more to it than meets the eye. It has the wrong initial for a start."

"Maybe he stole it and that's the initial of the original owner."

"That is always possible." Admitted Clara.

"Well, if nothing else it was vital for helping us identify Mervin."

"Yes, and that leads me to another thought. These thieves who tried to steal Hepkaptut, what if they also know that the ring identifies Mervin and they want to remove the evidence?"

"Because they killed him?"

"Perhaps so."

Oliver unfurled the umbrella, which was big and black, and held it over Clara.

"You will be careful, won't you Clara." He said, his face a picture of worry.

Clara gave an annoyed sigh.

"Why does everyone keep saying that?"

Chapter Thirteen

Dr Deáth liked his job. This came as a surprise to many people, not least those who his wife asked around for dinner. Sharing a table with a man who could quite happily talk about the various corpses currently in his morgue all night was not everyone's cup of tea. Deáth was aware he was, to put it politely, a little odd, but he saw no harm in this. In fact the number of bodies who came through his doors as victims of apparently normal people suggested to him that being run-of-the-mill was not all it was cracked up to be.

Deáth was forty-two, married to a delightful Quaker called Mary who appreciated his work, if not perhaps his conversation. They had no children, but Deáth consoled Mary this was just as well considering the amount of small children who perished through accident, injury and illness and ended up in his morgue. Perhaps, in the scheme of things, it was best to be spared such possible sadness.

He spent a lot of time in the morgue because there was always a lot to do. Not necessarily murders, in fact they were the tail-end of his trade. By and large he dealt with accidental or sudden deaths that needed explaining for the authorities. Many were the result of the burgeoning car market, but he also dealt with a fair number of poisoning mishaps, industrial tragedies and drownings. Being right next to the sea the latter was fairly common. However, the one thing Deáth could claim to have never seen before that week was a modern mummified corpse. Oh he had seen the ancient ones in the British Museum and like every other visitor he had gawked at men and women who had lived thousands of years before. But to see a man who had been alive only fifteen years ago perfectly preserved by natural means was a true novelty. Mervin Grimes had kept him occupied every waking hour since he had first met him at Clara's house. Mary was quite fed up of finding him in a daydream over his meals, mumbling about preservation and humidity.

Deáth was therefore rather glad to see Clara at his door, knowing that she at least would appreciate his ramblings about natural mummification.

"Miss Fitzgerald."

"I've been impatient and couldn't wait any longer to hear what you have found. I apologise for arriving so early."

It was nine in the morning and Deáth had been in the morgue since seven, using every available hour of daylight to get on with his work.

"Come in, would you like tea?"

As the kettle whistled in Deáth's office and he laid out a tea tray of mismatched cups, Clara made a pointed effort to not think about what was contained behind the many doors on the wall that looked like cupboards. In fact, she made a pointed effort not to think about any of the bodies lying around her.

"How goes the investigation?" Deáth asked as he absently removed a bleached arm bone from the tea tray, "I never know how these things end up there."

"It's slow at the moment. Too many suspects, not enough evidence. Mervin ran with some bad people, he might have gotten into a fight with one of them, or he could have been bumped off by a rival."

"Perhaps my report will help. Let me show you what

Mervin Grimes has told me."

They returned to the large hall of the morgue where six metal tables gleamed under the bright bulbs of artificial lights and the sunshine streaming in through high windows. Three of the tables were occupied, the unfortunates discreetly covered by white sheets. Deáth went to the nearest table and pulled back the cloth. Mervin Grimes grimaced at them in the only manner he was able to.

"Shall I start with the vital statistics of the victim?" Deáth asked.

"If you wish."

"Mervin Grimes, supposed age at death 23. Five foot, five inches tall, with slight bow legs that suggest rickets as a child. Well-nourished at the time of death, in fact there was the remains of a meal in his stomach, preserved like the rest of him. It was hardly digested, I would suggest it was something like chicken and potatoes. But that is only a guess."

"So he had a good meal just before he died?"

"Absolutely."

Clara made a note in her book and motioned for Dr Deáth to continue.

"Victim was in general good health, there were some indicators in his lungs that suggest he might have been in the early stages of Tuberculosis, but otherwise his organs seem healthy. They were all there, by the way, so no effort had been made towards his preservation like the Egyptian mummies. He had three silver fillings in his jaw and was missing another two, which were definitely lost before death. If you need extra proof of his identity then his dentist should be able to confirm what dental work Mervin Grimes had done." Deáth paused to take a breath, "There were no signs of a fight, so I would suggest he was not killed in a brawl or some similar skirmish. Nothing was broken and a minute examination of his skin showed no signs of cuts or other marks, except for this."

Deáth motioned to the ring finger on Grimes' right

hand.

"Take a close look at this finger."

Clara came close and peered at the blackened appendage. Deáth offered her a magnifying glass and she examined the skin carefully.

"There is a line near the knuckle?" She suggested.

"Yes, an incision. It looks as though someone tried to remove the finger, presumably to get the ring off."

"Colonel Brandt noticed that too. I imagine they were trying to remove the evidence of his identity." Clara said, "I wondered as much."

"Ah, but the wound has healed. The cut is not fresh but has had time to at least begin to repair."

Clara felt a little sick.

"That means someone tried to cut off his finger before he was dead."

"Yes it does."

Clara stared at the body, another part of Mervin Grimes' life had come into focus and it wasn't pleasant.

"Would you mind removing that ring from his hand Dr Deáth?"

"Of course," The coroner showed no concern about the request, but picked up a large pair of cutters, the sort Clara had seen used to remove thick chain, and set the blades over the finger, "You might want to shield your eyes. There is no knowing if he might splinter."

Clara put her hands protectively over her eyes, trying to block out the nasty clunk and breaking sound that accompanied Deáth's work. She would rather not think about fingers, even dead fingers, being removed. There was the sound of the heavy cutter being put down and a slight grunt from Deáth before he spoke again.

"There you go!"

Clara cautiously held out a hand, not sure if she was going to receive a mummified finger in it. Fortunately Deáth had had the sensibility to remove the ring from its dead digit. He dropped the large piece of jewellery in Clara's palm.

Clara could now take her first really close look at the ring. The first thing she noted was the S in the centre tended to warp with the light, at times not looking like an S at all. The second was that inscribed on the inside of the ring, where it was pressed firmly against Mervin Grimes' skin was minute writing that she found impossible to read, even with the aid of Deáth's magnifying glass. She placed the ring in her pocket.

"What about that bullet wound?"

"Ah, that is interesting too." Deáth went over to a side table and brought back a tray containing a shrivelled object much resembling dried tripe, which turned out to be Mervin's heart, and next to it a small bullet, "As you may imagine it wasn't easy extracting the bullet, I had to cut through the ribcage and very carefully disengage the heart from where it had stuck to the spine, but after all that I was able to get to the bullet. From an ordinary pistol I should say. It had pierced the left ventricle, there were several large blood clots and also dried blood in the chest cavity. I would say he died quite quickly."

"So he was definitely shot to death?"

"Absolutely. Oh, and from the way the blood has pooled and dried I would say that he was then positioned in an upright manner. My surmise is that he was concealed in a wall, propped up."

"How grim." Clara shook her head at the strange ways of humanity, "As awful as it sounds, were there any signs of torture?"

"No, why?"

"Just a theory, you see other members of the Black Hand were bumped off by a rival gang from London, but usually in a rather gruesome manner. The poor soul tortured and the body then left in a prominent position to be found."

"Well Mervin wasn't tortured. In my professional opinion he never saw the shot coming. He didn't struggle or fight, there were no signs of restraints and the pistol was probably fired pretty close to him."

"Very curious." Clara agreed, "At least I don't appear to have to go to London tracking gangsters."

"Oh I hope not!"

Clara took another long look at Mervin Grimes. His last hours on this earth had been a very mixed bag. One moment he was eating a pleasant meal, the next someone shot him. Her mind flashed to Penny Palmer, the girlfriend with a volatile temper. Supposing she had met Mervin that evening and they had fought, perhaps over the money he had won or the mysterious deaths of his comrades. Then she had taken leave of her senses and shot him. Finding Penny Palmer would certainly be an interesting part of the puzzle.

"Thank you Dr Deáth, as ever you have been most enlightening."

"I can only thank you for providing me with such an interesting corpse." Deáth grinned, apparently not aware of the strangeness of what he had just said.

Clara took her leave of him and headed out of the realm of the dead back into the August sunshine. She let the warm light fall on her face for a moment and then considered her next move. Tracing Penny Palmer might prove tricky. She may have returned to Margate, or she may have married and changed her name. But finding Mickey Walker should be relatively straightforward, as long as he hadn't moved away.

Clara found her way to the nearest post office and asked to see the directory for Brighton. She turned to the Ws and scanned down the names. There were several Walkers, but only one listed as Mickey. She noted down the address, then decided to test her luck and look up Palmer. It wasn't a great surprise when her search turned up no Penny Palmer; she had probably married at some point and taken on a different name. She handed back the directory and set off to find Mickey Walker.

Mickey Walker occasionally worked as a plumber, he also occasionally moonlighted at his brother-in-law's removals business, but more often than not he was to be found stretched out on the sofa in his front room doing nothing in particular. Mrs Walker regularly complained they had no money and Mickey would wander out and do a few odd-jobs for people to satisfy her. Then he would dump the money into her hand and return to his spot on the sofa. There he would lie for hours on end staring at a spot of damp on the ceiling. He knew every inch of that spot, but still it never bored him to stare at it. Mickey Walker, had he been educated enough to contemplate it, might have said it was his lack of imagination that was his greatest survival skill.

Clara knocked at a peeling door, down a rather smelly alley. There was a fat rat sitting boldly in the gutter, eyeing her like a watchdog.

"Who's there?" Someone called through the door.

"My name is Clara Fitzgerald, I wish to speak to Mr Walker about a missing person."

"What missing person?"

"Someone he used to know. Could I come in and talk, I won't be any bother?" Clara wondered if she really wanted to enter the house, which did not look promising from the outside, "Is he in?"

The person behind the door – a woman by the sound of the voice – shuffled about and seemed to be talking to someone in a low voice.

"Are you after money?" She finally asked.

"No," Clara thought fast, "But there is always a possibility that if Mr Walker was of great assistance in this matter the family might consider a reward."

The hint of money achieved exactly what Clara had hoped and the door opened instantly.

"You best come in then." Said a small woman who appeared to be dressed in clothes that were just one stage away from becoming rags.

Clara entered a dim hallway and took a better look at her hostess. She was a hard-faced woman with the sort of eyes Victorian novelists liked to call gimlet. She looked exhausted by life, the sort of exhaustion that takes years and years to build, but can never really be left behind. In her well-washed blouse and skirt, and grey apron, she gave the appearance of one of the street people in a Hogarth print. Mrs Walker wiped her forehead with the back of her hand.

"He's in there." She pointed to a closed door, "If you don't mind I'll leave you to it, I've got four more piles of washing to do before the day is out."

She gave a nod and then vanished down the dim passage into what was presumably the kitchen. Clara let herself into the room Mrs Walker had pointed out. It was a small front parlour, which might be politely described as snug. Everything looked tired and overused, from the faded rug to the green sofa, even the man who lay on the sofa looked like he had seen better days. Clara stepped into the room and almost trod on a small child who was playing with three wooden clothes pegs that had been crudely dressed and painted to resemble people.

"Mind yourself, thar." Mickey Walker called out, though he neither raised himself to move the child or help Clara into the cramped room.

Clara gave the child a smile and carefully lifted her feet over the sorry-looking dolls, managing to squeeze herself between an old round table and a black metal fireplace. There was no seat apart from the sofa Mickey Walker occupied so Clara assumed she would have to stand.

"I won't get up, me gout's bad today." Mickey said.

He was tall and lean, probably without his shirt on you would see his ribcage. His clothes, like that of his wife, were almost threadbare and one pink elbow was poking through his left sleeve. There was a dullness about him. Clara couldn't quite describe it, but it was somewhere between intense melancholy and soul-rending despair. His eyes stared at nothing and were dim, he clutched his hands on his paltry stomach and lay half turned from the window. He showed no interest in the child or her presence, other than to tell her he wouldn't get up.

"My name is Clara Fitzgerald." Clara held out a card, but Mickey didn't move, "I wanted to ask you about someone you used to know."

"I used to know a lot of people." Mickey said quietly, addressing himself to a sofa button.

"I imagine we could all say such, but this is a particular man who I am hoping you can remember. His name was Mervin Grimes."

Clara had half expected a reaction and for a second Mickey's hands twitched, then he seemed to press himself further into the sofa.

"Don't remember him." He said.

"I rather think you do. I was told you used to be friends."

"Someone is having a laugh with you."

"I don't think that is in Bob Waters' nature."

Mickey tensed.

"Is he that big boxing fellow?"

"Yes."

Clara waited. For a long time there was no sound except for the child clattering the wooden pegs together. Then Mickey turned his head a little towards her.

"Is Mervin alive?"

"No. He was shot fifteen years ago."

"I always thought he would come to a bad end." Mickey sniffed, "Why are you here then?"

"Because I have been asked to find out who killed Mervin and I am trying to trace people who used to know him. I was told to speak with you. I don't know if you are aware but a lot of the Black Hand gang came to rather unpleasant ends."

"1905 was a bad year for 'em." Mickey nodded solemnly, "They got too big for their boots and decided to take on the Paddington gang down from London. Mervin was a fool for such larks. He didn't like how the London boys came down here and swaggered about like they owned the place. He wanted to show them up."

"So Mervin was behind the race fixing?"

"It was his idea, yeah, and he persuaded the other lads to go along with it. The Black Hand was never a real, proper gang, you see. It was always a ragtag assortment of street boys and a couple of older blokes who had done time and knew what was what." Mickey licked his lips, "You said something about money?"

"That will depend on how helpful you are to me Mr Walker." Clara gingerly leaned back on the table, "Were you part of the Black Hand."

"Not really." Mickey snorted, "I mean, I knew Mervin and sometimes I did him favours, but that was as far as it went. I wasn't interested in being a full-time criminal and Mervin knew that. But I was useful to have around. I was a lot younger then and I had fast legs. I often ran messages for the gang."

"What about on the day they fixed their last race?"

"Oh yeah, I ran a message then. Ran several in fact." Mickey hoisted himself up a little on his sofa, "The police in Brighton were mighty hard on race fixing and the race bosses kept tight security. Night and day there were guards on duty, but Mervin had his ways around that. He picked one of his smallest lads, a reliable sort but small, like. He gave him a bag filled with bottles of beer and bread and cheese, and a blanket. Then the night before all the horses were due to arrive and race the lad snuck into the stables at the course and hid away in one of the unused storage rooms. So when the horses and the guards and the police arrived, ready to catch someone sneaking in, he was already there ahead of 'em. He slept and ate and pis… well you get my point, in that room. But it was all worth it, for just before the race he was able to slip out and dope the horses as he pleased. Then he went back to hiding in the storage room."

"I imagine the police and the race course bosses were not impressed."

"Nor were the fellas from London. On that day I took several messages between Black Hand members on the course and I went past those London gangsters more than once. Mean looking sorts they were. And they looked even meaner once they lost."

"Did they realise it was Mervin and the Black Hand who had tricked them?" Clara asked.

"Difficult not to the way Mervin crowed about it. He was a clever one all right, but he didn't have a lot of common sense. Me now, when I saw the way things were going I slipped out of the race course and never even asked for my share. When I saw what happened to the others I was glad I didn't." Mickey made a tutting noise with his tongue, "I think it was Reggie they got first, he was a bit like a lieutenant in the gang, but his weakness was drink and women. I doubt he was hard to find that night. He washed up on the beach the next morning looking like he had argued with a brick wall. Well, I think everyone's nerve cracked a little when they saw that. They knew at once it was a warning. And of course Mervin was already gone. Everyone expected for him to be washed up next. But he never was, was he?"

"So opinion within the Black Hand was that Mervin had been a victim of the London boys?"

"Naturally."

"Any idea what happened to his share of the money?"

Mickey propped himself up on one elbow and watched the child for a moment. He was clearly considering how much to say.

"The boys in the Black Hand didn't exactly go in for banks or savings plans. Most spent their money as fast as they earned it. Just as well for a lot of them, as they wouldn't have had the chance to enjoy it later." He didn't need to articulate that he was referring to the untimely deaths of many a Black Hand member, "Look, if you happen to find any of Mervin's winnings I want a cut for helping you. You don't look short of a penny, but me…" Mickey indicated his parlour, "I was part of that scam and I never got paid for my work."

"You said yourself you didn't hang around for your cut." Clara said coolly.

"That was self-preservation. No point getting the money and being too dead to enjoy it. But here I am, one of the few that are left, and I think I deserve my share."

"Are you suggesting Mervin Grimes stashed his money somewhere?" Clara asked cautiously, up until now there had been no hint that any money remained.

"Mervin liked his drink and his dancing, yeah, but he had his old mum to think of. He put a bit aside for her, in a secret place. She was supposed to get it if anything happened to him."

"Who knew of this place?"

"Not his mum, that's for sure. If she knew she would have hounded him for the money and spent it. No, as far as I know he only ever told that girl of his."

"Penny Palmer."

"Yeah."

Clara let this sink in, a new motive had just emerged.

"But if you knew of his secret stash, so might others?" Clara postulated.

"Oh no doubt, when Mervin had a few pints in him he was prone to bragging. He just kept quiet about the location. I reckon it was a locked box or something, he talked about a key once. Could be anywhere, of course. If he had any sense he buried it somewhere."

"Mickey, think carefully, if this box is still hidden somewhere, how much do you imagine would be in it?"

Mickey's eyebrows lowered as he considered the question, he tapped the fingers of his right hand on his flaccid belly.

"Wouldn't be surprised if there was something like £1,000 in that box."

Clara restrained herself from gasping. £1,000 was a lot of money, especially for someone used to poverty like Mervin Grimes, or for that matter his mother. If that box still existed all Mrs Grimes' woes would be at an end, at least financially. But where on earth had Mervin hidden his loot? And what was this key? Could it be that he had been murdered for it and the box had been emptied fifteen years ago?

"Mr Walker, I don't suppose you know what became of Penny Palmer?"

Mickey gave a shrug.

"I never got on with her."

Clara left the room, negotiating the obstacle of the small child and its peg dolls who, if nothing else, showed a dedication to its meagre playthings as resilient at its father's attention to the damp spot on the ceiling. She had just entered the hall and was debating if she would be in time to catch the omnibus home when Mrs Walker emerged from the kitchen.

"You won't forget us if you find Mervin's money?" She said quietly, with the desperation of the terminally poor.

"No Mrs Walker, I won't, but it is always possible Mervin was murdered for that money and it is already gone."

"I never liked him." Mrs Walker wrinkled her nose, "We all grew up in the same street, but he was always a trouble-maker. That ma of his could never see no wrong in him, nor that daft oaf Bob Waters. He was bad news. I'm glad he's dead, he would have led my Mickey into wicked ways."

"I'll keep you informed of anything I find out." Clara promised, "I don't suppose you know what became of Penny Palmer?"

"I didn't like her either." Mrs Walker puttered, "She thought herself better than the rest of us because her daddy worked in an office. She was from Margate, but I always thought there was something odd about the way she never went home. She said she was a typist and rented a flat with two other girls. Could be that was true. After Mervin died I deliberately lost track of her, but I do recall seeing her marrying someone in the papers. Must have been 1907 or '08. He was older 'an her. Think he had a P name too, bit like Peters. I remember thinking that at least she wouldn't have to worry about changing the initials on her handkerchiefs!"

Mrs Walker gave a hoarse laugh.

"I really hope she is quite miserable, like the rest of us!"

"Well thank you Mrs Walker." Clara let herself out the front door and found it was raining again. She had neglected her umbrella. Pulling her hat down over her ears she braved the downpour and only hoped Annie didn't see her coming home drenched – she would never hear the end of it otherwise.

Chapter Fourteen

The stationmaster's letter (on Liverpool Central headed paper) confirmed PC William's story. Jurgen Smith had bought a third class ticket for London and a second ticket from the Capital to Brighton. He should have arrived home in the early hours of Christmas Eve 1918. Only he never did. The stationmaster had been good enough to include details of the other ticket holders heading for London that day and Tommy noted that Dieter and Friger were among them. So what had become of Jurgen Smith?

Tommy put down the letter and picked up the phone again. For a housebound detective he wasn't doing so badly, though it helped that so far all the people he needed to speak to were on the phone. He knew his luck would run out eventually and it did when he asked the girl at the exchange if she could locate a Mr Friger living in Norwich. After a lengthy wait she called him back to explain that Mr Friger did not appear to be on the telephone. He then asked for a Mr Dieter in Surrey. The girl, who sounded a tad annoyed at this point, asked him to bear with her and rang off for yet another lengthy period. She finally called back to state there were three Mr Dieter's on the telephone in Surrey. She gave Tommy all their addresses and was then disgruntled when he said he didn't want her to connect him.

Tommy needed time to think and to consider what he would ask these strangers who may have nothing at all to do with Jurgen Smith. It may have been a complete fluke they got in the same carriage as him.

He was toying with his fountain pen, wondering if Friger still lived at the address he had given PC William, when Annie walked into the room. Annie was technically the Fitzgerald maid, but her role in the household was much more complicated than such a title implied. For a start her relationship with Tommy was teetering on the verge of becoming a full-blown romance. Not that either would admit to such.

"There's a man on the hall telephone who wants to speak with you. He says he's a brigadier. You aren't going back into the army, are you?"

For a moment Tommy couldn't tell if she was serious or not, he gave a glance to his legs.

"Well, if good old Dr Cutt fixes me up, you know…"

Annie gave him a mischievous smile.

"You better talk to him right away, he doesn't sound like the sort of man to keep waiting."

"He never was." Tommy said, "Wheel me through, dear Annie!"

They had just arrived at the hall stand where the phone perched when the front door flew open and Clara stepped in. She was a dripping wet mess. Annie gave out a gasp at the sight. Clara threw off her hat which was utterly ruined and would never sit right on her head again and pulled off her dripping coat.

"It's raining a bit." She announced to them both, "I'm going to have a hot bath."

She vanished upstairs before Annie could begin berating her for going out without an umbrella. The drama concluded, Tommy lifted up the ear piece of the phone and spoke into the receiver on its slender, pillar stand.

"Brigadier Beard, hello Sir."

Beard sounded impatient at the other end of the phone.

"You take a damn long time answering your telephone!"

"It isn't easy when one doesn't have the use of one's legs, Sir." Tommy said a little sharply, despite knowing he needed the brigadier on his side.

Beard huffed on his end of the line but made no comment.

"I had a look at those papers for you." He said after a sufficient period of stormy breathing had passed, "There was quite a file on your fellow Smith."

"Really?" Tommy was genuinely astonished.

"He was an agitator, nothing serious, but one of those sorts who can't keep their nose out of trouble. He was always trying to get extra privileges for the internees and stood up for a couple of fellows who got themselves into trouble. There were all manner of letters and petitions in his file, here, this one for example. 'Mr Jurgen Smith, courteously requests that men of no denomination are not excluded from the Easter celebrations, but are included in such events as the Easter supper and Sunday cricket match. It has come to his attention that certain authorities have expressed a wish for these to be exclusive for those who attend the church service on that day, which would be detrimental, in his opinion, to morale among the men.' There is a lot of stuff like that, you get the picture."

"So Jurgen was an advocate for his fellow internees?"

"He was a damn nuisance if you ask me. Why can't people just get on with being held prisoner and stop bothering the chain of command? Do you know how much paperwork that causes?"

Tommy could guess.

"Aside from these letters, was there anything that hinted of more sinister trouble in Jurgen's life?" He changed the subject.

"Nothing that stuck out, he seems the sort who everyone liked. Oh, but that other name you gave me,

Dieter, he was a real trouble-maker and was even once under suspicion for murder."

"What a minute... Alphonse Dieter was a suspected murderer?"

"Seems like a fellow was drowned in the harbour, might have been an escape attempt. In fact that's what the guards on the island assumed at first. But when the body was hauled out of the water the deceased had a nasty gash on his head and finger-marks around the throat. The theory was someone had attacked him, tried to throttle him and then either pushed him into the water and in the process he banged his head, or banged him on the head first which caused him to tumble off the harbour wall." Beard cleared his throat and there was a rustle of papers, "At first no one seemed interested, then a local came forward and described seeing two men standing at the harbour wall around midnight the night before. It was a strange sight to see because mostly everyone was in bed by then, and the authorities were not keen on lights being shone at night in case of an enemy zeppelin spotting them. Naturally with hardly any light it was difficult to describe the men, but he swore that he could hear them arguing and one used the name 'Alphonse.'"

"Dieter's name was Alphonse."

"Yes, but I presume you are aware the name is Old German and not so uncommon? In any case there were too many 'Alphonses' on the island to focus in on one and the local had not actually seen anything occur other than an argument. However, the victim was a known braggart and was generally disliked, particularly by this Dieter fellow, who had some sort of disagreement with the victim." Beard shuffled more papers, "The authorities suspected Dieter and your chap Smith stood up for him, wrote some quite heated letters on the topic. The case could not be proved, in fact there was hardly any evidence. The authorities pressed hard on Dieter trying to get a confession and that got Smith into battling mode. He complained to everyone there was to complain to."

"Was Dieter ever arrested?"

"No, but the files suggest he was, and still remains, prime suspect for the killing. It's always possible he didn't just stop at this fellow in the harbour."

Tommy had to admit that was a possibility. If he was hot tempered and had argued with Jurgen Smith, was it possible he had killed him?

"Was there anything on Hans Friger?"

"Only basic information."

"And there was nothing that might suggest a reason for Smith disappearing?"

"He probably drove the British army lads insane while he was being guarded, but there was nothing to suggest anyone would want to kill him. He doesn't seem to have been in any trouble and as far as the Isle of Man authorities were concerned when 1918 came he was sent home and that was an end of it."

"Thank you for your help, Sir. It is much appreciated."

"We are even now Fitzgerald, understand?"

"Yes Sir."

"Good, take care of yourself private."

"You too Sir."

Tommy replaced the ear piece of the phone, waited a moment then, with a slight pang of nerves, asked the exchange to put him through to one of the phone numbers listed under the name Dieter. His first call put him through to an elderly man who was extremely deaf and who needed Tommy's question about whether he knew Jurgen Smith repeated three times, before he was able to give a sharp 'no' and slam down the phone. The second Dieter was actually a woman who had failed to correct her phone directory records after the death of her husband. Neither had been interned during the war. It was the third Dieter that finally gave Tommy some good news.

"Yes, I knew Jurgen."

"Are you sure we are talking about the same Jurgen Smith?"

"Tall, dark, a bit of a goody-two-shoes when he felt like it. That Jurgen."

"That's the one. I am looking for him."

"I can't help you then, I haven't seen Jurgen in two years." Alphonse Dieter sighed heavily on his end of the phone, "You should try his mother in Brighton."

"That's just the thing, she doesn't know where he is either."

There was a long silence on the line.

"Who is this?" Dieter asked with a hint of unease in his tone.

"My name is Thomas Fitzgerald, I am investigating the disappearance of Jurgen Smith on behalf of his mother."

"Why are you calling me?"

"Because, from what I understand, you may be one of the last people to have seen him. You boarded a train with Jurgen in 1918 after leaving the Isle of Man?"

"I suppose I did."

"What happened after that?"

"Jurgen got off the train in London, what happened after that I don't know."

"Jurgen definitely got off the train at London?"

"Yes, I just said! Look, I haven't seen him since we parted ways in London two years ago." Dieter gave an odd cough, there was a clattering noise in the background as if wherever he kept his phone was in a busy place with people around, "Look… has someone… have you been speaking to the Isle of Man authorities?"

"Should I be?"

"Have you, or haven't you?"

Tommy considered the implications of the question, then said very calmly.

"They told me about the murder."

Dieter swore quietly under his breath.

"I didn't kill anyone, hardly knew the man."

"That isn't why I am contacting you." Tommy assured him.

"No? But you suspect me of killing Jurgen, yes? They say I killed once before, so maybe I killed again?" Again Dieter swore to himself, "Reuben van Cole, that was the name of the man who fell in the harbour. He was in his forties, a part-time drunkard with a habit for bragging that got on everyone's nerves."

"You disliked him?"

"I wasn't alone! Anyway, some interfering soul reckoned he had heard my Christian name being called and told the authorities. As it happened the day before I had confronted van Cole for taking my pocket watch. He was a thief among other things. I had put the watch down when I went to wash. I knew he had taken it because I saw him leaving as I came to put on my clothes. We argued over it, I insisted on searching his room and there was my watch. He tried to deny it, but the watch was engraved. I punched him. That was it, it was all over."

"He didn't start the argument again the next day, perhaps?"

"No! I just happened to have been the last to argue with him, that's all. Plenty others had argued with him too, and several were called Alphonse, if you want to believe that witness."

"Shouldn't I believe him"

Dieter grumbled something, then said;

"He didn't exactly like Germans."

"But Jurgen was on your side?"

"Jurgen was on everyone's side, he was like that. I'm sorry, I sound angry, but it is not with him. Just... just with all that time I spent for no good reason on an island. Jurgen somehow managed to stay positive, I hated him for that. Not to want to kill him, he was a friend. He just annoyed me sometimes."

"I believe you Dieter."

There was a pause.

"You do?"

"Yes."

"I wish I could help you find Jurgen, but we parted

ways at the train station. I was heading for Surrey, he was off to Brighton to see his parents for Christmas."

"During the train journey, did he talk much or about anything in particular?"

"Jurgen liked to listen to others more than talk. He did seem extra quiet that journey now you mention it. Like something was on his mind. I remember he fell asleep and we had to wake him at the station. We all stumbled off and Jurgen looked dead on his feet. Hans Friger was going to take him for a cup of tea before the next train. I had to make a fast connection so I left them. We said goodbye and that was that."

"So I can't ask you if Friger stills lives at the same address in Norwich either?"

"No. I'm sorry. I put that part of my life behind me. I didn't want to stay in touch and be reminded."

"One last thing, is there any reason, anything at all that you could think of that might explain Jurgen simply vanishing after he got off that train?"

Dieter said nothing for a while, he was obviously thinking. The clatter in the background resolved itself into the noises of children playing.

"Jurgen wasn't the sort to just vanish. He wanted to go home." Dieter sounded quite upset, "All this time I imagined he had got back to Brighton and had a happy Christmas with his parents. Instead, he was just, gone."

"I'm going to find out what happened." Tommy promised, wondering if he could keep his word.

"When you do, could you write to me and tell me?" Dieter was plaintive, "I don't want to sit here thinking over all the possibilities."

"I shall do that." Tommy answered.

He confirmed Dieter's address and then put the phone down. There was a great deal to think about. His last hope was Hans Friger. He had the address Friger was returning to in 1918 and he just had to hope the German was not inclined to move house. After speaking with Dieter Tommy was once more convinced that Jurgen had not simply decided to vanish, something had happened to him. It might have been an accident. Perhaps he was just another of the casual victims of mishaps in London, knocked down by an omnibus, trampled by a taxi. In the dark days of December London streets became treacherous. Had Jurgen become just another of the unidentified lost souls the Metropolitan police picked up deceased every day after an accident? Buried now in some pauper's grave because no one could identify him? Or had something much worse happened to the man who was on everyone's side? Tommy hoped not, somehow an accident seemed preferable to the thought of Jurgen being murdered for his wallet. What of this Hans Friger? He had caused no trouble during his internment, but did that mean anything? Who was to say what he was like or what he was capable of? Had he taken an opportunity when Dieter had turned his back?

Tommy didn't like any of those questions, nor the answers they suggested. But he had started this search and now it had to be ended. He would write to Hans Friger and hear what he had to say. If there was any chance, no matter how small, that Jurgen was still alive then Friger was his best chance of finding it. If not, Tommy wasn't sure what else he could do.

He listened to the rain hitting the front door and a shiver went down his spine.

Chapter Fifteen

Clara did not often bemoan the state of marriage (though in her experience it resulted in a few more corpses then was perhaps comfortable), however it did annoy her immensely that when a woman got married she changed her name, thus rendering her almost impossible to find. Unless you knew who she had married, of course. Clara did not know who Penny Palmer married, so it was with a touch of despondency that she went to the local newspaper office and spent most of the afternoon trawling through the announcements in additions of the Brighton Gazette from 1907 and 1908. It was a long search, but it produced results. On 24 December 1908 Miss Penny Palmer married Gregory Patterson, a bookseller. A grainy photograph showed husband and bride in the church doorway. Both were smiling at someone behind the photographer's shoulder. Penny looked older than the twenty years the newspaper claimed she was, but then Gregory looked younger than the thirty-nine he was listed as being. Clara studied the picture a little longer, trying to get inspiration about the character of Penny Palmer through printed black lines of ink on grey paper. She gave up the exercise as futile after a few moments.

The next stop, now this elusive information had been discovered, was the post office where Clara could see a current copy of the town directory. She turned to the list of Ps in the trade section (as Gregory was listed as selling books, so logically owned a shop) and gave herself a surprise. For Gregory Patterson was the proprietor of Brighton Books, the very shop Tommy was always visiting to pick up pamphlets on American detectives and criminal investigation. Clara closed the directory with a sharper thud than she meant and the postmistress glowered at her over her spectacles. Clara gave a smile then hastened back into the street.

It looked close to rain again as she found her way to the high street, negotiating afternoon shoppers and children currently released from their schooling for the holidays. Several people were talking about the fair; Clara caught snippets of conversation, including the tail end of a sentence declaring the police had had to be called again after some trouble arose. Making a mental note to talk to Inspector Park-Coombs next time she had the chance, Clara spotted Brighton Books and darted in the doorway. She collided with a rotund grandmother carrying an armful of books, while her small grandchild squalled at her side that they weren't the books he wanted. Several books fell to the floor and Clara earned yet another reproving look. It really was not her day.

Safely in the shop Clara took a moment to grasp her bearings. She couldn't recall the last time she had entered this place; though she liked to read she rarely had the time and when she did she could always find something in her father's library to work through. It was obvious other people did not have the same problem, for there were several customers scattered about the towering bookcases that reached up to the ceiling, browsing in that respectfully quiet manner only found in places where the printed word was sold (excluding newspapers, of course!).

Clara made her way to the counter in the centre of the shop, behind which a bald gentleman with half-moon glasses smiled at her. Mr Patterson had not aged so well in the last 12 years, time had finally caught up with him and his face looked tired. His dark hair only remained in thin wisps behind his ears and in the moustache over his upper lip. He had thin, artistic hands, with long fingers that were always on the move. He was lean and slightly hunched, possibly because he was a tall man and had spent all his life trying to pretend he wasn't. He had a nice smile though and spoke very gently, despite a bad fitting denture giving him a lisp. This was the man who had won Penny Palmer's heart? It somehow beggared belief that such a quiet soul had taken a shine to a woman that the rest of Brighton considered a thieving vixen with little in the way of morals. Still, it took all sorts, Clara supposed.

"Mr Gregory Patterson?"

"Indeed, my dear. How can I help you?"

"Actually I was looking for your wife Penny. Is she in?"

Mr Patterson's smile tightened.

"My dear, you are five years too late. I'm a widower."

Clara had one of those moments when she wished a huge shaft would open beneath her and swallow her up.

"I'm sorry, no one told me that." Clara bit at her lip, wondering what else she could say.

"May I ask why you wished to see her?" Gregory Patterson asked in the same manner he might use when enquiring about a book a person desired.

"It was not anything important, not now. It was about someone she knew fifteen years ago."

Patterson tilted his head on one side. A quizzical look crossed his face.

"I don't suppose that would be Mervin Grimes, would it?"

Clara managed to hide her surprise.

"Actually, yes. I didn't realise you were aware of him. His body has finally been found after all these years and I am trying, on behalf of the family, to discover what happened back in 1905. I thought Mrs Patterson might be able to help."

"I'm sure she would have liked to, had she been able." Patterson looked at his watch, "It's very close to closing time. Might I ask you to bear with me while I shut up the shop and then we can chat?"

"If you wouldn't mind?"

"Not at all, please go through the brown door at the back of the shop marked private where you will find a sitting room. I shall join you in just a few moments."

Clara followed his instructions and found herself in a rather old-fashioned parlour. Crocheted blankets were draped over the backs of old leather armchairs and the mantelpiece was adored with a velvet cloth. She peered into a glass dome containing dried flowers and a taxidermy frog, decided it was a bit too grim and turned instead to the narrow window which looked out into a side alley. The room was naturally dark, but a gas fitting in the middle of the ceiling fed into a three-prong brass light, with opaque domed glass shades. Gas light casts a unique sort of light, one filled with flickering shadows. It all made Clara feel rather oppressed. Had Penny once sat in this room and contemplated the gas light? Had she crocheted those blankets in her spare time? Or stared at the frog in his glass dome with the same distaste as Clara?

She was startled when Patterson opened the door.

"Would you mind if I just change into my slippers? My feet get so swollen in my work shoes." He said, closing the door behind him.

"Of course not."

"Thank you, may I offer you tea?"

"There is no need to bother on my account."

"Thank you." Patterson lowered himself into one of the armchairs with a groan and slowly worked off each of his shoes, exchanging them for red tartan slippers, "Growing old is an unremarkable business, but it is very depressing. This shop, for one thing, seems to become more wearisome each year that slips by. Never a day off, except Sundays and Christmas, never a holiday. I daren't be ill, who would pay the rent? And at the end of the day what do I have but an empty house and a cold hearth."

"I'm sorry to hear that."

"I doubt I am alone, Mrs..?"

"Miss Fitzgerald. I could come back at a better time if now is inconvenient."

Patterson lightly smiled.

"There is no better time. You reach a stage in your life when you stop expecting to wake up in the morning with nothing aching. Instead you are grateful when it's only the knee that aches, or only the back that twinges. Still, at least I see people every day. Some folks don't have even that."

"My brother is very fond of your shop." Clara decided it was time to move the conversation off such depressing topics as aging and ill-health.

"Is he now? What books does he prefer?"

"He is very fond of true crime, I do believe he has ordered a number of detective books from you. I recall one in particular about the experiences of an American private investigator."

"Ah, yes, I know your brother! He certainly has diverse interests. Did the volume on poisons suit him? It was a challenge to find."

"He found it very useful." Clara said, wondering why all her conversations were so strange, "I wish I had more time to read myself."

"As amusing as it sounds for a man who works in a bookshop, so do I!" Patterson laughed, "I'm surrounded by the written word all day long, yet my own literary tastes are sadly neglected. Many evenings I sit here and wish I had the money to retire."

Somehow the topic had come round on itself, so Clara once again tried to push it on.

"Did Penny like books?"

"Penny was not the reading sort. She was helpful in the shop, but I could not enthuse her with literature. A shame really, but I suspected as much when I married her."

"How did you come to meet?"

"Penny was a typist, I employed her. At the time I was attempting to put together a catalogue of this shop. I bought it fully stocked from an elderly gentleman who was moving to live with his daughter in Devon. He had never kept a written inventory and I found myself with 1,500 books and not a clue as to what any of them were. The process of cataloguing is tedious at the best of times, but especially when you don't know what you are doing. I contacted a secretarial agency and explained my problem. They sent me Penny."

"She was good at cataloguing?"

"She had the mind for it. She arranged things alphabetically by author and also by subject. She gave each entry a description and even referenced other relevant works. There was a non-fiction and a fiction catalogue. My shop has never been so organised since. I employed her for a week and on the last day I asked her to dinner. After a month I asked her to marry me. I didn't fool myself to think she loved me. But she was sad and lonely, just like me, and it seemed better to be sad and lonely together."

Patterson's eyes crinkled as his mind flicked back through the years, his smile became winsome as he drifted into nostalgia. A tear formed at the corner of his eye.

"Turns out Penny was more lonely and sad than I realised."

"What happened?" Clara asked, sensing she was on delicate territory.

The old bookman blinked back his tears and found a handkerchief in his pocket to clean his glasses. It seemed a long time before he answered.

"Penny gassed herself. Put her head in the oven. I was away in London at a book fair. I've never forgiven myself for not being here with her."

"People do things sometimes, that we…"

"Please, no platitudes Miss Fitzgerald, I have heard

them all. Penny waited for me to be gone, I appreciate that, it does not change the fact that if I had been here it wouldn't of happened."

"Maybe she would have jumped off a bridge instead?"

Patterson gave a little start.

"That wasn't a platitude." Clara said gently.

"It certainly wasn't."

"Other than being unhappy, was there any reason for her actions?"

"You mean, did she have a guilty conscience over something?" Gregory Patterson shook his head, "Nothing like that. Penny was always dwelling in the past, but only because she believed she had been happier then."

"When Mervin Grimes was alive?"

"When she was young and everything seemed full of promise. And, yes, I suppose Mervin Grimes was a part of that." Patterson's tone had grown harder, less sorrowful, "That young man had filled poor Penny's head with ideas of luxury and wealth beyond her dreams. And she believed every word. How can you go from that to working in a book shop? I used to try and convince her that Mervin had been a big talker, nothing more, but she didn't take to that idea. She was certain the night he disappeared he had been coming to get her so they could marry."

"Why did she think that?"

"Because it was better than imagining he had disappeared with all the money he won that night and left her behind."

"So she told you about the race fixing?"

Patterson shrugged.

"We had no secrets and she was not directly involved. She told me a lot of things."

"All about Mervin's schemes?"

"Yes."

"What about his enemies?"

Patterson cocked his head, like he had in the shop. Clara took it as a signal he was thinking.

"I don't recall her mentioning any names. Naturally there was all that trouble with the London gangsters. Penny told me how scared she was at the time. She even went to Mervin's mum, asking if she knew where he was. His mum said he had gone off to Newcastle, of all places, and that was that."

"Did Penny believe her?"

"She didn't see eye-to-eye with that woman. No, I don't think she did."

"Do you recall her ever mentioning anything about a key?"

"No."

Clara felt the threads she had neatly gathered together, once again falling into a jumbled mess.

"Is there anything else, anything at all, you recall her saying about Mervin Grimes?"

Patterson mused on this, he stretched out one sore foot.

"She liked to go to the old church in the fields at Hove, is it St Andrews? Anyway, she liked it there because her and Mervin used to sit in the graveyard. Back then the door to the crypt was not kept locked and Mervin had a fascination for sneaking in and looking at all the long-dead bodies. Penny said it was creepy, but Mervin liked the dead. They told no tales, as the saying goes. Penny never joined him, but afterwards… well, she was always in that graveyard and church."

Clara considered the irony of this story. Here was Mervin fascinated by corpses residing in a crypt, finally ending up in a similar situation and fascinating crowds across the country. Fate has a sense of humour, it seemed.

"You said they found the body? Where is it?"

Clara glanced up, surprised by the question.

"I couldn't say."

"Have you seen it?"

"Briefly."

"Was it wearing anything?"

Clara narrowed her eyes.

"Grimes was unfortunately quite naked, what is your interest Mr Patterson?"

Patterson shook his head.

"I'm merely curious." He gave a smile, "Would you ever so mind if we ended our chat now? I do feel rather tired and I must get my supper on. You are always welcome to return."

"Thank you Mr Patterson if I think of anything else…"

"Don't hesitate to call, good day Miss Fitzgerald."

Clara found herself back on the Brighton high street, a deep sense of unease stirring in the pit of her belly.

Chapter Sixteen

The following Sunday Tommy was surprised when Clara insisted on attending church, though not just any church, but St Andrew's Old Church in neighbouring Hove.

"Why? Not that I'm not delighted you are taking an interest in religion, you understand." He asked.

"I want to look at the crypt and thought it best to catch the vicar while he was about."

"I should have known it was all to do with dead people."

"Isn't everything?" Clara asked in surprise.

St Andrew's had been built in the Twelfth century, which meant by the nineteenth it was in serious need of renovation. Its tower had fallen down in 1801 and by 1833 it was in serious danger of being completely demolished. But Hove residents could not quite resign themselves to seeing the old church gone forever, so it was repaired and in parts rebuilt until the glorious edifice, with turreted Gothic tower, reopened in 1836. It looked a strange collaboration of old and new as Clara and Tommy approached, but the ancient stonework had accepted its modern square tower with grace and the whole seemed to have settled into the landscape. It certainly seemed a peaceful place.

"Stop right there!" Tommy cried to Clara as she

pushed him up the path, "Look at that grave."

Clara glanced to the side and spotted a headstone.

"George Everest." She read out loud.

"Sir George Everest, you know who he was, yes?"

"Of course Tommy, he was the first person to determine the exact height of Everest, hence its name."

"Precisely. Who would have imagined he was buried here?"

"I hope Mervin Grimes was not attempting to view his dead body. Seems rather sacrilegious."

"That's a strong word from a heathen like you." Tommy grinned at his sister.

She stuck her tongue out at him.

They had timed their arrival to coincide with the end of the service and the congregation were streaming out into the warm sunshine, shaking hands with the vicar as they went past. Clara waited until it seemed almost everyone was gone then approached the priest.

"Reverend Hancock?" She enquired.

The reverend was an older man who had the appearance of a benign vulture. He was a man who had settled into the routine of his duties at St Andrew's very much as the church had settled into its footings. Outside of his pastoral and spiritual duties very little troubled him, in fact he was proud to declare to anyone who cared to listen that he only had a vague idea of who was now leading the country, though he could list the complete and current hierarchy of the Church of England, alphabetically. He gave a smile to Clara which provided her a glimpse of his rather large over-bite.

"Good morning, I'm afraid you have missed the service. There is another this evening at seven o'clock."

"Thank you, actually I wondered if I might ask some questions about the church?"

Reverend Hancock took a good look at the new arrivals, he was not a man for history and considered the one penny guidebook available at the back of the church an adequate way to answer such questions. He was about to mention it, when Clara added.

"In particular I wanted to ask if your crypt is accessible to the public?"

Hancock gave her a strange look.

"Your interest is?"

"It's rather peculiar, but I am investigating the death of a young man who apparently was fond of visiting a particular church. I believe it was St Andrew's, but it will depend if you have a crypt. You see this young man was fond of going down into it."

"That sounds very odd."

"Doesn't it? He was an odd man. Tragically he was murdered."

"That is deeply distressing, but sadly the crypt beneath St Andrew's has been inaccessible for several decades."

"Oh." Clara was thrown, she had been certain St Andrew's fitted the bill perfectly.

"There must be somewhere else." Tommy said, "Unless Penny Patterson was telling her husband lies about visiting a church."

"Penny Patterson?" Reverend Hancock had given a start, "This is connected to Penny Patterson?"

"Yes, rather it is." Clara saw she had gained the vicar's attention, "I take it you knew her?"

"Penny was one of my regulars, until her unfortunate passing." Hancock looked uncomfortable, "Exactly who has been murdered?"

"His name was Mervin Grimes, before she married he was Penny Patterson's boyfriend."

Hancock gave an understanding nod.

"Oh, I have heard that name before." He rubbed at his vulpine chin, "Perhaps you would come inside and we might have a chat? Perhaps I was too hasty earlier."

Reverend Hancock helped Clara pull Tommy's wheelchair over the step that led into the church and found them a quiet spot in a pew to the far side to talk. There were still a handful of people in the church putting hymn books back in their places, tidying the flowers and generally tending to the orderly appearance of the building. Hancock placed his guests as far away as possible so they would not be overheard.

"Would you mind telling me what you know about Penny Patterson?" He asked.

"As I said before she used to walk out with Mervin Grimes. Then he disappeared, or rather, as we now know, he was murdered, and she married Gregory Patterson the shopkeeper. Other than that she was a typist, I know very little about her." Clara explained.

"Penny Patterson was one of those people you have a feeling about." Hancock perched himself in the wooden pew, facing Clara and Tommy, "The sort of person you know is not going to have a happy ending."

"From what I gather she was a very unhappy soul."

"Unhappy, self-destructive, you name it." Hancock shook his head, "I dare say her husband tried to help her, but he was not very effective. Though I suppose in the long run, nor was I. She sometimes cleaned the church, it was almost like a penance to her. She told me once how she used to come to this church in the evenings with Mervin Grimes. They would act rather disgracefully in the graveyard, sometimes in the church too, if it was open. She regretted that, felt she had committed a dreadful sin."

"Did she tell you about Mervin Grimes?"

"She told me he was a bad lot, but she loved him too much to care. They had made all sorts of plans together, all Mervin had to do was make his money. She never forgave him for disappearing."

"Did she say what she thought had become of him?"

"She had been told he went to Newcastle. She said at first she refused to believe it, but as the years went by it started to seem more likely. To the very last she imagined he would come back for her." Hancock leaned back in the pew and reflected mournfully on the past, "I never expected her to kill herself, at least, that's what I have told myself all these years."

"Did you ever learn why she did it?"

"I imagine it was a combination of things, she was very depressed those last months. She could see no future for herself, just an endless existence of working in her husband's bookshop. She never had any children. As I said before she was riddled with guilt, some days she was convinced Mervin had vanished because of something she had done and nothing I said could change her mind."

"What had she done that could drive him away so dramatically?"

"Penny used to drink, I say used, I suspect it was still a problem for her, but she concealed it well. Once, when she was drunk, she told some of Mervin's friends, or rather, members of his gang, about a stash he kept. She told them it needed a special key to find it. It was a big secret and she always felt revealing it had forced him to leave. Her logic on the matter was rather tenuous, admittedly."

"Mervin Grimes did store his money somewhere," Clara said carefully, "And money is a powerful motive for murder."

"Then, perhaps that is why Penny blamed herself for his disappearance?"

"I have to ask, Reverend Hancock, but in your opinion could Penny have killed him?"

The reverend gave a slight laugh, tossing back his head and exposing his ill-fitting jawline.

"Penny was no angel, but she would never harm anyone." Hancock paused, "You mentioned Grimes' fascination with the dead? I want to show you something."

He led Tommy and Clara back outside to an old stone vault. A statue of a weathered knight with a shield stood guard at the front, while the rear portion of the tomb had almost vanished into a dense bank of ivy.

"This is the family vault of the Seylons. I am reliably informed the first Seylon came over with William the Conqueror. The tomb is not as old as that, more seventeenth century. The last Seylon was buried in it in 1883. I want to show you this." Reverend Hancock pushed his way into the ivy and indicated that Clara should follow. Tommy sat in his wheelchair, indignantly looking on, "When the last Seylon was interred, Joshua Romulus was his name, it came to the attention of my predecessor that the family vault had not withstood the test of time as well as it might."

Hancock pushed back the ivy in handfuls and revealed what at first appeared to be a darker patch of stone, but resolved itself into a large, vertical hole in the back of the vault.

"When the vault was opened it was discovered that the rear slab had almost completely crumbled away. It looks like shoddy workmanship, or perhaps the stone used here was of an inferior quality. In any case, by the time of Joshua Romulus' death the Seylon family fortunes were in a dire state, there was barely enough to bury him, let alone carry out repairs. The church made enquiries of his nearest relatives, but they showed no interest. The decision was finally made to allow this ivy to encase the tomb and so hide the fallen wall. But as you can see, a person could enter if they so chose." Saying that Hancock stretched out an arm and hauled himself into the gap. He vanished in a rustle of ivy.

Clara stared at the space where the reverend had been, knowing full well she had to follow. She took a deep breath and thrust herself into the vault. The space inside was far from huge, a little too tight for two people and almost completely dark. Clara had to bend over to avoid cracking her skull on the roof. As her eyes adjusted to the light, what little there was, she made out the remains of coffins sitting two abreast and stacked one on top of the other. The lower coffins, presumably the oldest, were bulging and broken. Their sides falling apart and bones protruding, the weight of those on top crushing them down. The most recent coffin was a mahogany one with gold fittings, sitting across two other coffins at a right angle. Clara assumed this was the coffin of Joshua Romulus.

"If, as you say, Mervin Grimes came to St Andrew's to look at the dead, then this is where he would come." Hancock said.

Clara found the whole idea appalling, but then again she was not a gangster. With some difficulty she found the hole again and dragged herself out. Hancock followed. He pulled the ivy back into place and the hole vanished once more.

"Penny always showed an interest in this tomb, which is why I thought of it." He said as he rearranged the tendrils of ivy.

Clara returned to Tommy.

"So, does this help us at all?" He asked.

"In terms of finding Mervin's killer, not really."

"Had you noticed that?" Tommy pointed at the knight on the vault. It held a large shield that was clearly once painted, but time had worn the colour almost completely away. Still, there was the faintest of hints of blue on the stone. Right in the middle of the shield was a stylised S.

"Remind you of anything?" Tommy remarked, "It does me, but then I've been staring at it for five minutes."

Clara pulled Mervin's ring out of her pocket and looked at it.

"Oh don't tell me…" She held up the ring next to the shield, "Oh lord, he did! He stole it off a corpse!"

"It bears the insignia of the Seylon family."

"Probably came straight off Joshua Romulus' dead finger." Clara felt disgusted, "Mervin Grimes was a very disturbed young man."

"You could always return it now?" Tommy suggested.

Clara admitted that would be the sensible and decent thing to do, but something made her hesitate.

"There is more to this ring than just that it came off a corpse." She said, "Someone tried to cut it off Mervin while he was still alive and those thieves at the fair were after it. It means something, or at least they think it means something. So I'll hang on to it until I figure out what exactly that is."

Tommy gave a nod and then his stomach grumbled and his thoughts turned to more practical matters.

"Fancy seeing if that pub we passed on the way here does lunch?"

"I don't think I could eat after what I saw in that tomb."

"A missed meal will do you know harm."

"What are you implying Thomas Fitzgerald?"

"Nothing, dear sister!" Tommy grinned, "Just maybe you should lay off Annie's puddings for a while."

"Just remember who is pushing your wheelchair." Clara said with a mock scowl.

Chapter Seventeen

What with lunch (a pretty decent ploughman's) and several glasses of quality ale (for Tommy), it was getting late in the afternoon by the time they reached home and Clara was considering settling down in her favourite chair to look through the newspaper with a cup of tea when she entered the front door. She had barely taken off her coat when Annie hurried up to her.

"There are two gentlemen waiting for you in the front parlour. They've been here over an hour." She said.

Clara glanced at Tommy, then back at Annie.

"Who are they?"

"Well, one is that police inspector, the other had a very peculiar name which I don't dare pronounce in case I get it wrong."

Clara hung up her coat.

"I better see what this is all about."

She went into the parlour and found Inspector Park-Coombs sipping tea and eating a fruit scone, while next to him sat the permanently jovial Dr Deáth. Clara completely understood why Annie was afraid of saying his name.

"Good afternoon gentlemen, what brings you here?"

Inspector Park-Coombs put down his teacup.

"There is a mummy in the morgue." He said sternly.

"I believe we were both aware of that fact." Clara responded, hooking a chair away from the parlour table and turning it to face her two visitors before sitting down, "Is he causing a nuisance?"

Deáth chuckled to himself.

"You might say that."

Clara looked at him quizzically.

"There was an attempted break-in." Park-Coombs clarified, "Some fellows were after our good friend Mervin Grimes. We suspect they are the same chaps who have been causing bother at the fairground."

"Ah, three men, two older, one younger?" Clara said.

"As usual you appear to know what's happening at my own police station." Park-Coombs answered with more than a hint of sarcasm.

"I spoke with the gentleman in charge of security at the fair and that was his description of the culprits."

"The question is," Deáth's glasses sparkled in the late afternoon sunlight, "why do they want his corpse?"

"My first thought was they were trying to take the body before it could be identified and cover up a murder. But after this length of time I rather suspect it is more a case they are after this." Clara reached into her pocket and drew out the Seylon ring.

"Grimes' ring?"

"Not just any ring Dr Deáth, rather ghoulishly it came from a corpse prior to it adorning Mervin Grimes' finger. Joshua Romulus Seylon's finger to be precise. He is buried in a vault at St Andrew's Old Church in Hove. His resting place is sadly falling to pieces and it appears Grimes learned how to slip inside."

"Why doesn't it surprise me he would steal from a dead man?" Park-Coombs sighed, he had long ago concluded the criminal mind would sink to any depths.

"The thing is inspector, this ring seems to attract a lot of attention. Someone wanted it badly enough to try and cut it off Grimes' finger before he was dead. It's a pretty bauble, but not worth that much effort unless it has another importance."

"Like?"

"Many of the people I have spoken to keep telling me that Grimes had a secret stash, a nest-egg hidden somewhere. There was a key to it, now you could take that as a literal key, for instance to a safety deposit box. Or you could take it metaphorically." Clara turned the ring over in her hand, "Had I more nerve this afternoon I might have taken a closer look at Seylon's coffin to see if Mervin left us any other clues there."

"I think you should come to the station Miss Fitzgerald." Park-Coombs abruptly stood up.

"Right now?" Clara said in astonishment.

"I want to break these thugs, so far I can't get a peep out of them. Maybe that will change when they see that ring."

Clara sighed.

"I'll get my coat."

Clara had not been in the interrogation rooms of the Brighton police station before, but she was unsurprised to find them rather plain with barred windows and a single table in the middle. Park-Coombs offered her a chair while they awaited the arrival of the first prisoner.

"I'm aiming for the weakest link first." The inspector commented as he made himself comfortable as best he could in his chair, "His name is Sam Fawkes, small-time thief. I think we've arrested him four, no, five times over the last few years. Nothing spectacular. As far as I am aware he works to his own tune and doesn't run with any gang."

"He is the youngest of the trio?"

"Yes, and, in my opinion, the most scared of the lot. He hasn't been out of prison all that long and he is not keen on going back."

"Then he shouldn't commit crime, should he inspector?" Clara pulled the ring out of her pocket and placed it on her finger, "I do apologise Mr Seylon for using your ring, but it is for a good cause."

"Are you talking to the dead, Miss Fitzgerald?" The inspector said with a smirk.

"It is invariably more satisfying than talking to the living." Clara shrugged.

The door rattled and Sam Fawkes was half pushed through the door. He did look, as the inspector had remarked, scared. Clara tried not to let her softer side feel sorry for him as the police constable shoved him into a chair opposite the inspector.

"Ah, Mr Fawkes." Park-Coombs rested his elbows on the table, "Still sticking to your story that you only accidentally broke into the police morgue?"

"Billy was sure as sure can be that that was the basement we had been told to clear out on account of this old dear dying and no one leaving a key. We had to break in, was just the wrong door."

"Naturally Mr Fawkes. Did it not trouble Billy that the 'basement' did not appear to be attached to a residential property?"

"Billy never was good at addresses and stuff."

"And when we found you opening the doors to the little compartments where the bodies are stored?"

"They looked like cupboards all right." Sam gave a little shiver, "Look, do you think I would have gone into a morgue on purpose? I'll have nightmares for weeks."

"You are a good actor Mr Fawkes."

While the two men chatted Clara had placed her hand bearing the ring casually on the table. Sam had not appeared to notice it.

"What were you really looking for, Mr Fawkes?" Clara asked to draw his attention to her.

Sam looked at her as if he had not been aware of her presence.

"Wasn't looking for anything. We do house clearances, that's Billy's line of business."

"Rather appropriate for a burglar." Park-Coombs said.

"He's an honest man, is Billy Brown." Sam staunchly defended his friend.

A bell rang in Clara's head.

"His name is Billy Brown?"

"Yes?" Sam looked at her as if this was a trick question.

Clara gave the inspector a look but said no more.

"Ever heard of Mervin Grimes, Mr Fawkes?" The inspector continued.

"No."

"He vanished in 1905."

"I was just a wee nipper then, you can't pin that on me."

"No, quite." Park-Coombs rapped his fingers on the table, "Are you sure I can't persuade you to sell out your colleagues? Really, it would not be beyond you."

"Inspector!" Sam gave an almost genuine look of horror, "I am an honourable man!"

"Yes, and I'm a monkey's uncle." Park-Coombs waved a hand at the constable by the door and Sam Fawkes was removed from the room, "So Clara, what was that look for?"

"Billy Brown. I mean there could be more than one, but Billy 'Razor' Brown was one of the Black Hand gang. In fact he is down in your police file as having been murdered by a rival London gang in 1905."

Park-Coombs thought about this.

"I couldn't say how they made the identifications."

"But say this is Billy Brown, a surviving member of the Black Hand, one who was thought dead. Could it be that he had an interest in murdering Mervin Grimes for his share of the money?"

Again there was a lengthy silence as Park-Coombs considered this idea.

"Even if he didn't, he might have learned about Grimes' stash." Theorised the inspector, "And he would be in the perfect position to identify the corpse from the ring."

"And to know the ring was the key to Grimes' hidden loot."

Park-Coombs started to grin.

"Let's have a word with Mr Billy Brown."

Billy 'Razor' Brown was a man of hard edges and sharp corners. There was no softness about him, no gentleness. He walked into the room like a man prepared to fight anyone who looked at him wrong. He had no shame about being in handcuffs nor, clearly, any remorse. He sat at the table, his arrogant, lined face sneering at them. He had nasty, black eyes that pierced into a person. Clara took an instant dislike to him.

"Razor Brown." Park-Coombs said calmly.

"Who?" Billy said without emotion.

"I apologise, I was informed your surname was Brown." Park-Coombs said without looking up.

"It is, but I ain't heard of this Razor fellow." Billy snarled.

"Well, it has been fifteen years." Clara interjected, "I wonder if Mervin Grimes' mother would recognise you?"

"Who's the bird?" Billy assessed Clara with icy eyes. She noted they flashed briefly onto her hand and took in the ring.

"Morgues, Mr Brown, let's concern ourselves with them." Park-Coombs changed the subject.

"I don't know anything about morgues." Billy snorted.

"You were in one today."

"I mistook the address, it happens."

"You appear to mistake addresses quite frequently Mr Brown. A dozen times in the last five years to be precise."

"Do you ever get to London these days, Mr Brown, or do you prefer to avoid the Capital?" Clara dug in again, "I know some find the people there rather unwelcoming."

Brown gave her a wicked look that must have scared more than a few people witless in their time. It certainly gave Clara pause for thought.

"Are you one of these women police? I don't hold with women doing that malarkey, you should be at home looking after a husband."

"I prefer not to take advice from criminals." Clara

responded.

"If you were my woman, I wouldn't let you talk like that!"

"Mr Brown, can we return to topic?" Park-Coombs' rapped the table with the intended result of Brown's eyes once more being drawn to the ring, "Why were you in the morgue?"

"I was lost."

"You were looking for the body of Mervin Grimes."

"No I wasn't."

"Yes, you were, just as you were looking for it in the fairground."

"Why would I want a body?" Brown grunted a laugh.

"Mervin Grimes was not a friend of yours?"

"Never knew the man." Brown folded his arms and sat back in his chair, "You have nothing on me."

"Except your presence in the morgue." Park-Coombs reminded him.

"Won't stand up in court, I was lost."

"You really are a very arrogant man." Clara said abruptly, annoyed with the creature before her.

"Don't she talk fancy?" Brown grinned at her, it was not nice, "What's your name, darlin'?"

Clara did not reply.

"Mr Brown, you are mistaken. I have a good case against you." Park-Coombs waved for the man to be taken away.

Brown threw them both a sneer as he left, and winked at Clara.

"He was horrible." She said as the door closed.

"He doesn't know who you are Clara, and he is safely trapped in the cells here."

"Thank goodness for that." Clara groaned, "He noticed the ring."

"I saw that, I think you are right and he wants it. I don't think he killed Grimes though."

"No?"

"He was clearly too busy making it seem as if he was

dead, so as to avoid being killed by the London gangsters he and the Black Hand had diddled."

"So who did they kill?"

"Another member of the Black Hand, probably someone we had no file on. Or some dupe Brown came across." Park-Coombs shook his head, "You would be amazed what a man with no conscience can achieve."

"What about the third man?"

"I don't think it's worth bothering. They clearly have their stories straight. I'll let them stew for a bit then try again. I still think Fawkes is our best bet."

"Then might I go home and enjoy the last part of my Sunday?"

"That you may, Miss Fitzgerald."

Clara went home but she was worried. Things didn't feel right, she had answers, but not the right questions. The murderer of Mervin Grimes was proving just as elusive as ever. Supposing, she asked herself, it had nothing to do with the Black Hand or its criminal activities? Where did that leave her? Penny Palmer? No, that didn't fit. So who was left?

She arrived home and fully meant to relax for the few hours that were left in the afternoon, but first she had a letter to write. She grabbed some paper and a pen and hastily scribbled out a note;

"Dear Mr Donovan Ruskin…"

Chapter Eighteen

Monday morning brought a policeman to the doorstep. Clara didn't recognise him, he looked fairly new and rather shame-faced.

"Can I help?" She asked, wondering if the inspector wanted her to return to the station.

"I've come to deliver a bit of bad news, the inspector says not to worry, but last night Billy Brown escaped."

Clara felt her heart beating faster.

"How?"

"Don't know miss. The inspector is raving about it. No one can say how Billy got the key to his cell." The policeman suddenly brightened, "Don't you worry, we'll nab him soon enough. His sort don't go far."

Clara thanked the policeman for his optimism and quietly closed the door. She was very still for a moment. Then she went to the parlour, wrote out a note, and called for Annie.

"Annie dear, please could you deliver this."

Annie took the note and read the name and address on the front.

"I was going to take the post after dinner."

"I rather feel this needs to be taken now, please." Clara said, masking as much of her anxiety as possible.

"I'll just pop my hat on then." Annie eyed Clara suspiciously, then vanished.

Clara paced the parlour for a moment after she had

gone. Then she went to the dining room and sat at the table. Scattered around her were various things she had written on the case at hand, and it had been her plan for the morning to go through everything and see if she could start making sense of the matter. Now she felt too distracted to concentrate.

Outside it was a warm, sunny day. Clara would have liked to retire to the conservatory to enjoy the sunshine while it lasted, soon the taste of autumn would be in the air. Instead she rested her elbows on the table and placed her head in her hands, for a while all she did was sit there like that. Then she made a decision. She stood and grabbed a poker from the fireplace. Returning to her chair she carefully laid the poker on the seat beside her.

Midday came and went. Tommy had another appointment with Dr Cutt and Clara made a fuss about Annie going with him. They both seemed to notice her agitation, but couldn't understand the cause. She was relieved when they left.

Clara sat at the dining room table and placed Mervin Grimes' ring (or rather Joshua Romulus Seylon's ring) before her. It was an ugly thing. She was beginning to doubt the stone in the middle was a true sapphire, or for that matter anything valuable. It had the shiny quality of cut glass. Having spent the morning going through her father's old books on the peerage, she could hardly imagine the ring was anything more than a cheap bauble.

The Seylons had once been powerful and rich, the sort of powerful you get from being chummy with royalty and the sort of rich you get from crushing the poor underneath you without any qualms. But they had also been Catholics; all very well until the turbulent years of the Reformation when kings and queens changed the country's religious preference faster than you could say Mass. The Seylons hung on to their old faith with the doggedness they had once been famed for in battle. On this occasion it served them badly. The country became Protestant and Catholics were under threat. The Seylons had made dangerous enemies and the next century saw them fighting a losing battle to keep their lands and power. By the time things had settled the Seylons had lost most of their fortune and had returned to a crumbling mansion in the countryside around Hove. There Joshua Romulus grew up and eventually died. The last of a long line who knew the type of poverty only the formerly rich can know. As he watched each year pass, he ignored the old house crumbling about his ears and took solace in the old Seylon library (which he bequeathed to Brighton) spending his time compiling a rather dull and long-winded volume on the family. As luck would have it Clara's book-obsessed father had a copy. Though the densely printed pages did not tell her anything useful for the case, they did at least pass the time and Joshua had rather helpfully inserted an engraved portrait of himself on the front page. There he sat, staring at the reader sadly, a large ring on the hand he rested on the arm of his chair. Proof, if ever Clara needed it, that this was his ring.

She turned the ring over in her hand. It had obviously meant something to Joshua, perhaps a relic of the past? Something he could use to conjure memories of happier times. The last of the Seylons had died leaving nothing but debt. Within a decade of his death the old mansion had collapsed into rubble, helped here and there by local builders salvaging what they could. And then one day a boy had crawled into the old family vault to gawp at the corpses and in the process stole Joshua's ring.

Clara closed the book on the Seylons, deposited the ring in her pocket and paused. There was the faintest of sounds coming from the hall. Had she owned a cat or dog Clara would have put the noise down to the animal moving about. She owned neither, which meant there was no reason for the noise. Clara did not rise from her seat; instead she opened her book and pretended to read. The creaking noise sounded again. Empty houses were surprisingly good at carrying sounds, Clara concluded. She stared hard at the picture of Joshua Romulus, her heart starting to pound harder and her breath coming faster. The dining room door flew open.

Clara raised her head and looked across at Billy 'Razor' Brown. She had positioned herself near to the window but facing the door. Billy took a step into the room and stood at the diagonally opposite corner of the table.

"I was expecting you." Clara said calmly.

Billy gave an unpleasant grin.

"A little bird told me where you lived."

"And I imagine you want this?" Clara drew out the ring and placed it on the table.

Billy's eyes went to it at once, then he looked at her.

"Give it to me and I won't hurt you." He said.

"I hardly believe that." Clara sighed, "Besides, I am rather annoyed at having my house broken into. I presume you came though the conservatory?"

"I levered up the window." Billy cackled with pride, "Took me a while to do it quiet like."

"What a shame, I left the door unlocked for you."

Billy's smile evaporated.

"You think you are right clever, don't you?"

"Next to you?" Clara gave him an assessing look, "Yes, rather."

Billy flicked out a hand. There was a cutthroat razor in it.

"I was going to be nice, now I think I won't. I'll be taking that ring now."

"Do you even know what to do with it?" Clara asked, not moving from her seat.

"I'll figure it out, or maybe you'll tell me after I take that smile off your face."

"Were you the one who tried to cut this off Mervin's finger?" Clara waved the ring at him.

"Mervin was never good at sharing." Billy laughed, "A razor has a lot of uses if you can just get a man drunk enough!"

There was a sudden yell. Billy cried out as a large

body smashed into him and pinned him onto the table.

"You would hurt my poor pal Mervin?" Bob Waters shouted in Billy's ear.

Billy gave a yelp then he flung back his hand and slashed Bob's arm. Bob's grip on him loosened and the gangster jumped up to face him. Clutching at his bleeding arm Bob moved back a pace. Billy snarled at him and leapt forward, swinging out with his razor, scattering Bob's blood on Clara's wallpaper. Bob tried to tackle him, but the strength had gone out of his injured arm, and the pair wrestled for barely a moment before Billy was free again and dangerously close to cutting Bob's throat.

"You were always a fool Bob! Mervin used to laugh about you!" Billy cried.

Clara raised the poker in her hand and slammed it down hard on Billy's head. There was a dull thud. Billy staggered forward, his mouth a gaping 'O' of surprise. Then he slammed face first into the floor.

He awoke half an hour later with a very sore head. His first reaction was to raise a hand and inspect the painful spot on the back of his skull, but his arm wouldn't move. He tried to lift the other arm but that was equally immobile. It was then his senses regrouped enough for him to understand he was tied to a chair. He opened his eyes to see Clara standing over him, her arms folded and the poker still in one hand. Bob was just behind her with his arm bandaged and in a makeshift sling.

"I really do not like being threatened in my own home." Clara told Billy sternly, "So this is the deal, you answer my questions and then I call the police."

Billy snorted at her derisively.

"That's hardly a bargain."

"You misunderstand me." Clara tapped the poker against her arm lightly, "The faster you answer my questions, the faster you will be safely back in the hands of the police and away from me."

Clara pointed the poker at Billy's weasel nose.

"I have a very bad temper at times." She waggled the

poker and Billy found his eyes irresistibly drawn to it.

"You won't do anything." Billy said.

"Won't I? What exactly is that bruise on your thick skull Mr Brown?"

"You won't torture me." Billy pulled at his ropes, "Isn't your style."

"Maybe she won't." Bob Waters moved behind Clara and towered over Billy, "But I owe you one for Mervin."

Bob's hand moved fast and he punched Billy before the man had a chance to react. Billy gave a groan as his head went back and the room spun unpleasantly. When his vision restored itself he was feeling less self-assured.

"What do you want?" He asked, painfully aware that Clara was tapping the poker again.

"What happened to Mervin Grimes?" Clara asked.

"I don't know. We split after the race fixing. Them Londoners were after us."

"How were you still a part of the Black Hand after having tried to cut off Mervin's finger?"

Billy made a hissing noise.

"Mervin didn't remember who was around the night I almost had his finger. He was so drunk that night. Only reason I didn't finish the job was the bone was tougher than I thought. Should have used an axe."

Bob's fist swung out again, fast, and Billy whimpered in pain.

"Don't do that!" He whined, "Miss, call the police, please miss, before this madman kills me."

"So when did you last see Mervin?" Clara ignored the plea.

"At the race track, he was off home. That was the last time, I swear!"

"Now what about this ring?" Clara held up the piece of jewellery that had caused all this drama, "Tell me why it is important?"

"Mervin had a secret stash where he kept his money." Billy talked fast, "The ring is the key. Once you have the ring you can open the stash. Penny got drunk one night and told me."

"Do you know where the ring comes from?"

"Mervin bought or stole it, I reckon." Billy struggled with his ropes, "Let me go!"

"Not yet, it was the ring that led you to identify king Hepkaptut as Mervin, yes?"

"Yes! Never expected to see that ugly mug again!"

Bob reacted before Clara could stop him. Billy reeled and moaned.

"Now, I think, is the time to call the police." Clara told Bob, and the big man reluctantly left.

Alone with Billy, Clara stared at her would-be attacker.

"If you ever dare come back here…"

"I won't!" Billy insisted.

"Just say, you do. I won't hesitate to do more with this than just knock you on the head." Clara indicated the poker, "I am a reasonable person, but I won't be threatened, do you understand?"

Billy nodded miserably. His head hurt in a strange way, like someone had stuffed it full with cotton wool, then shaken it up, before smacking him between the eyes. It was hard to imagine that the small woman before him had done that much damage in one swing. Billy had been in a fair few pub brawls in his time, but never had his head throbbed like this. Nor had he ever seen someone so furious with him that it burned deep in their eyes. He had absolutely no intention of ever coming back to this house. For that matter, he never wanted to see Brighton again.

Bob returned.

"Police are coming."

"Thank you. I suggest we keep Mr Brown tied up until they arrive, just in case he thinks about escaping and I get the urge to use this again." Clara patted her poker.

Billy spent the next twenty minutes anxiously awaiting the arrival of the police. It was a first for him. He was tremendously relieved when Inspector Park-Coombs entered the house and glowered at him.

"She hit me with a poker." Billy said in a voice that sounded so plaintive and pathetic it made him ashamed of himself.

Park-Coombs tutted.

"Mr Brown you are under arrest yet again. Should you fail to obey me this time I'll let Clara loose on you, she looks about ready to beat nine bells out of you."

Billy whimpered again. Two police constables worked for several minutes to undo the knots Clara had so efficiently tied. Then they picked a rather shaky Billy up from his chair and half hauled, half helped him out the door.

"Sorry about that Clara." Park-Coombs said as soon as they were gone, "I'll find out how this happened and heads will roll."

Clara gave no answer, she was still brimming with pent-up fury, about ready to explode at anything. The inspector said his goodbyes and left. It was all Clara could do to close the door without slamming it. She found herself in the hallway trembling all over.

"Are you all right?" Bob asked gently.

"Yes." Clara answered stiffly, "I've just never been so angry before. I really feel I could have killed him and not even cared."

Bob gave a nod.

"Yes, but that's what makes me and you different from poor old Mervin. We resist that feeling." Bob took her arm softly, "I'll make us some sweet tea."

It was just on 4pm when Tommy arrived home. He entered the house unaware that for two hours that afternoon it had been the scene of such turmoil. Only Annie sensed that something was off, yet even she could not understand how dots of red paint had managed to stain the wallpaper in the dining room.

Chapter Nineteen

"Dr Deáth, thank you for meeting me here." Clara held out her hand to the doctor.

They were in the graveyard of St Andrew's Old Church. The weather was threatening rain and Deáth had come over in his old horse and buggy.

"I am really quite intrigued to see what is inside this vault." He smiled.

Clara found the doctor's constant enthusiasm a rare shaft of light on what had been a rather dark few hours. She was still shaken from her experiences with Billy Brown the day before.

"Do you know anything about the Seylon family history?" Clara asked as she showed him the vault.

"Not really, though I have dabbled in Brighton history. I don't suppose any Seylons have come through my doors?"

"No." Clara assured him with a smile.

She pushed away large clumps of ivy until the hole in the vault was revealed.

"Do you have that lamp, doctor?"

Deáth held up an oil lamp and carefully lit its wick with a match. He passed it to Clara, who shone the light into the hole. She could just make out the edges of the coffins.

"It's a bit cramped inside, I'll go first." She said lifting a foot into the gap.

She braced her hands on the stone sides, a brief thought flicking through her mind that if the back wall could crumble down, so could the ceiling, perhaps while she was inside. Knocking the thought away she pushed and pulled her way into the vault.

With the lamp lighting up the corners it seemed even more tomb-like than before. The hard stone sides were uncarved and tendrils of ivy had slipped inside and were slowly working their way around the dead. Various species of spider had nested in the corners for generations and quivered on their webs in the bright light. The coffins themselves looked in a worse state than Clara had remembered. The bottom pair were virtually crushed along with their occupants, though a few stray bones had apparently been pulled free by mice or rats and now littered the floor. The next coffins up looked little better and when Clara accidentally brushed her hand against one it felt sodden with water. In fact the whole place smelled decidedly damp and the green mould growing along the ceiling confirmed her suspicion that no one had bothered to make the place water-tight.

Deáth clambered through the hole spryly and took in the whole abode. He picked up a bone from the floor and examined it for a moment.

"Human toe." He suggested, before dropping the bone and wedging himself next to Clara, "So this is Joshua Romulus?"

He indicated the top coffin.

"I presume so, he was last in after all."

"Let's see, old fella, if you are missing a ring." Deáth pressed his fingers into the thin gap between the edge of the coffin and the lid. Years of damp had softened the wood considerably and it began to crumbles as his fingers dug in. It took no effort to lift the lid. The nails were long gone.

Joshua Romulus grinned at them from an open-mouthed skull. His clothes were still there, a fine black suit and carefully polished shoes, but the flesh of the man had long ago disappeared. Deáth reached for a skeletal hand that fell apart as he touched it.

"No ring." He said.

"What is that under him?" Clara had spotted a rip in the lining of the coffin and something narrow slipped into it.

Deáth had to rip the cloth a bit more to retrieve the object which turned out to be a box.

"Locked." He said, "It needs a combination."

"Let's take it outside, I can't stand it in here any longer."

They re-emerged into the daylight, Clara highly relieved to be back out in the open. How Mervin could ever have enjoyed being in that vault she failed to understand. Deáth gave the box a good shake as he stood in the open air. It rattled a little, but seemed too light to contain much.

"If this is his stash I would say your friend Billy Brown would have been disappointed."

Clara gave a snort at the name.

"Do you have any idea of the combination?" Deáth continued.

"Not really, I'm losing my patience with Mervin Grimes."

Deáth gave the box one last shake then came to a conclusion. He went over to the churchyard wall and picked a rough-cut stone in its surface that had a good point to it. Then he hammered the box against it with rhythmic, loud thuds. The box had suffered from the damp like the coffin and it only resisted for a few moments before the lock smashed into pieces and the front panel fell off. Deáth paused. He took off his jacket and spread it on the ground before emptying the contents of the box onto it. As he had suggested the stash was not promising. A rusty pair of keys flopped onto the jacket, followed by a note written in badly faded ink. Clara picked up the note and examined it.

"That's Penny's name." She pointed to a word at the top of the sheet, "Something like, 'Penny if you find this...'" Clara tried to make sense of the almost vanished words, "I think Mervin left this to give Penny an idea of where his stash was kept. I guess he didn't trust Joshua to be a good enough guard."

"Does he explain where?" Deáth asked.

Clara ran her finger over the paper.

"Look at that word, isn't it 'hall'?"

"It could be, this line here says something about ruins."

Clara's mind went back to those old books she had been reading yesterday.

"The Seylon family home fell to ruins after Joshua died."

"So perhaps Mervin stole more from the old boy than just a ring?"

"This bit here, it looks like the word 'cellar' and could this be 'north corner'?"

"Invariably when a house falls to ruins it is the cellar that lasts best." Deáth noted, "If it doesn't get filled in, then it will remain there indefinitely."

"The Seylon hall, I do believe, is just a few miles off. I was reading a book Joshua published on the family history only yesterday and he mentioned how St Andrew's could be just seen from an upstairs window."

"Let's take my buggy and see if we can find it." Deáth said enthusiastically, "I do hope old Joshua doesn't haunt the place."

He gave a laugh.

"Personally, I am more concerned about getting wet again." Clara sighed.

"A little rain never hurt anyone." Deáth reassured her as he led the way back to his horse and buggy. They managed to make it inside just in time to avoid the rain that pounded down on the old Seylon vault and dripped onto the bones of old Joshua.

Tommy had been left at home while Clara went on her mission and was in the process of deciding whether he should keep his collection of cricketing cigarette cards or whether they would serve a better purpose on the fire, when Annie tapped at the parlour door.

"Tommy!" She hissed, "There's a foreign fellow on the doorstep asking after you."

Tommy was puzzled, he had not been expecting anyone. But if someone had asked after him it was impolite to refuse them entry.

"Send him in Annie." Tommy said, closing the cigarette card album and wondering just who this might be.

Annie disappeared and a moment later a tall, lean man appeared in the doorway. He looked nervous. He was somewhere in his forties, with fair hair, a downward pointing nose and narrow lips. Though his appearance was hardly handsome, his bearing gave him a certain air of dignity that could be deemed attractive.

"Thomas Fitzgerald." Tommy offered a hand.

The visitor took it and shook lightly. His fingers were cold.

"Hans Friger." He said.

Tommy would have been hardly more surprised had the man announced himself as Jurgen Smith. He stared at the individual before him, trying to work out how this had occurred.

"You wrote to me." Hans said agitatedly.

"Yes I did. I didn't expect you here though."

"I felt it was important I come."

"Perhaps you best take a seat, Annie will be making tea as we speak." Tommy motioned to the armchair by the fireplace.

"Here, I brought this with me." Hans handed over a large parcel wrapped in brown paper and string as he took his seat, "You'll want to give that to Jurgen's mother."

Tommy found himself staring at the parcel. He quietly put it on the table then looked back at Hans.

"Is he dead?"

"Yes."

Tommy nodded. He had thought as much.

"What happened to him, if you know?"

"I know." Hans sat awkwardly in his chair as if ready to spring up at any moment, "I was there."

"Then perhaps you could explain it to me?"

Hans ran a hand over his face.

"You know we all got on the train at Liverpool?"

"Yes." Tommy said.

"Jurgen, myself and Alphonse. We were all headed for London first, then to get our connecting trains. Well Jurgen and Alphonse anyway, I was going to stay in London over Christmas with my sister. She is my only family in this country."

Tommy indicated he understood but didn't try to interrupt, he could see Hans needed to talk.

"I only knew Alphonse a little, but Jurgen and I had become friends over the years. Have you spoken to Alphonse?"

"Yes I have."

Hans fell silent, his hands folded in his lap, his eyes wandering about the room as if trying to find something to focus on.

"Alphonse is not the easiest of people to like. But Jurgen was. Jurgen was good to talk to, he listened. I found my years of confinement very hard. He made them easier." Hans rubbed at his lips, his hands were trembling, "Jurgen was very excited to be going home, he wrote a postcard to his mother which he posted at the station before we left. He kept talking about his mother's goose and Black Forest gateaux, until Alphonse was quite sick of it all and told him to shut up. I assumed that was why he seemed so quiet later on. It was late, anyhow, we mainly slept those last few hours."

Hans blew out his cheeks, seeming to be building up

his courage to speak further. Tommy remained patient.

"We arrived in London at about 3 in the morning. It was foggy and cold." He started again slowly, "Jurgen complained of feeling like ice was running down his back. Alphonse said he had slept awkwardly with his head against the window and that was the cause. We stepped out onto the station platform. Jurgen seemed groggy and almost fell. He complained again of being so cold. But his overcoat was worn and he had no gloves, so we weren't surprise. We decided to go for coffee and that seemed to help us all. Jurgen livened up a bit and was talking again. They put out an announcement that Alphonse's train was about to depart. Alphonse leapt up and raced out, barely saying goodbye. I remember Jurgen standing to shake his hand and when he sat down again he looked deathly pale. I asked if he was all right and he said he felt rather faint.

"I bought him something to eat. I think it was a pork pie. He ate slowly, but he didn't look right. I touched his hand and it was clammy. I said did he still feel like ice was pouring down his back? He said no, he was very warm now." Hans started to bite at the edge of his finger, "There was another announcement, Jurgen's train was ready to board. He didn't even move. I said, have you not heard, your train is ready? He just shook his head. Then he went to stand and almost fell. My legs feel like iron blocks, he said to me. I had to put an arm about his shoulder just to help him stand. I wasn't sure what was wrong just then, but he was obviously ill. I thought maybe he had caught a bad chill in the train. He had slept with his forehead pressed against the window and it had been so cold. I helped him back onto the platform, but he was in no fit state to board a train. I doubted he would even notice when it stopped."

Hans had chewed his finger so hard there was blood at the edge of the nail.

"I made the decision to take him to my sister's house. It would only be for a few days, I said to myself, just until he was better. My sister didn't live so far away, but it seemed a long walk that night. Jurgen complained of a headache and wanted to keep sitting down. I made him keep walking, I thought it was for the best…"

Hans stopped, staring at the bloodied finger as if he didn't recognise it as his own.

"Hans, before you continue, do you blame yourself for Jurgen's death?" Tommy asked gently.

"I blame myself for many things." Hans groaned, "But I don't think I did right by Jurgen."

"I can't comment on that until you finish your story, but so far you sound a considerate friend."

Hans timidly shook his head, denying Tommy's words.

"I should have realised how sick Jurgen was sooner." He said, his voice tight, "I helped him to my sister's house, he was like a block of ice when we reached the door. No sooner had I woken my sister and she let us in Jurgen collapsed. I explained as hastily as I could and we got him up to bed. He seemed feverish though complaining of being cold, so my sister soaked a cloth for his forehead and I rubbed his hands and feet to try and bring the warmth back to them. Then I went to my own bed and must have slept until midday.

"When I woke my sister said Jurgen was no better. It was Christmas Eve and she had her children downstairs decorating the house with paper chains and angels. I went in to see him. He looked at me and recognised who I was, he just couldn't remember how he came to be in that bed. After I explained I said should I call a doctor and he said no, he was feeling a little stronger. He would rest and then try and catch a train to Brighton that evening. He thought, like I did, that he had caught a chill.

"The day wore on, I helped the children make party hats for the next day. Jurgen slept mostly. When evening came it was clear to us all he could not head for Brighton. My sister insisted he stay put in that bed and brought him a supper of soup and good bread. He didn't seem any worse and we were sure he would be well enough to travel on Boxing Day.

"Only… Christmas Day he was so much worse. He burned with fever and was delirious. He kept saying how his head hurt and his arms and legs. We tried to send for a doctor but it was Christmas Day…"

Hans stopped again. His face had taken on a haunted look, Tommy had never seen a man look so grief-stricken in his life. The burden of guilt Hans had piled on himself was greater than anything he deserved, as far as Tommy could see.

"Finding a doctor to attend him on Christmas Day must have been almost impossible." Tommy said sympathetically.

"Especially when you are German." Hans replied, though there was no real resentment in his tone, "Of course, no one understood then about the influenza epidemic that was about to hit us. Such a blow after the war. I wonder sometimes why God felt the need to punish us so?"

"I tend to take the more pragmatic view that these things just happen."

Hans gave a small nod.

"It was nearly 7 o'clock when we finally found a doctor. He was not so bad, though he blustered and moaned about his Christmas dinner being spoiled. He said Jurgen had the flu and he needed rest and fluids. Then he left and said he would be back in the morning. I suppose he was busy, because it was not until the day after Boxing Day that he returned. By then Jurgen was hardly with us. He woke maybe once or twice to take a little drink of beef tea, then he would slip away. We didn't need the doctor to tell us it was a very bad case. He explained how the flu hit people in different ways and some just didn't seem able to fight it off. It looked like Jurgen was one of those sort." Hans stared at his hands, plaiting his long fingers together, "Jurgen died on 28 December 1918. The doctor signed a death certificate and advised us to bury him swiftly. I went through his few possessions looking for some clue as to his family, but there was nothing except a photograph of his parents. He had said they lived in Brighton, but there are an awful lot of Smiths in Brighton and I did not know their first names. Eventually my sister said we must bury him properly and hope that somehow we would one day find his family. Leave it in God's hands she said. So I did, and now here I am."

Hans went quiet. The clock on the mantelpiece ticked round a full minute (Tommy counted the seconds) before he spoke again.

"I would like to meet Jurgen's parents and explain."

"Only his mother is still alive." Tommy said, "I shall send for her at once."

Annie arrived with the tea things, she looked curiously at Hans as she placed the tray on the table. For a moment she paused, then she grabbed up a plate with a small cake on it and placed it in Hans' lap.

"It's a Duchess Bun, my mother's recipe." She said, "I hope you will eat it all up, you look as though you could do with a good bit of cake inside you."

Hans' slowly raised his eyes to meet hers.

"You are very kind."

"Oh, it don't take much kindness to offer a bit of cake. But you do look a sad soul. Have you come far?"

"Norwich."

"And have you settled on a place to stay?"

Hans indicated he had not. The unspoken statement, that he had not the money to afford a place to spend the night, was recognised by them all. No doubt he would have whiled away the night hours drifting between doorways and benches.

"Now here we have a spare bedroom." Annie continued stoutly, "And it don't take much more kindness for me to offer it to you, does it not Tommy?"

Tommy grinned at her, because it was very plain he was not being asked permission, but rather was being advised of the situation.

"I shall get out some fresh sheets and you shall spend

the night here, Mr..?"

"Hans Friger." Hans gave a quick bow of his head from his seated position.

"Well Mr Friger, I am Annie and I take people as I meet them. Now eat up your cake and I hope you like dumplings with your dinner."

A faint smile blossomed on Hans' face as Annie left the room once more.

"It is best not to say no to Annie." Tommy explained, "And she is a mean hand with her dumplings."

"I like English dumplings." Hans said, "And I like English hospitality."

"Well I hope you don't mind, but you may find here we run by 'Fitzgerald hospitality', which tends to mean once we nab you, you won't get away."

Now Hans laughed, it was a good sound and it seemed to surprise him.

"I really thought it would be awful coming down here."

"You've still got to face Mrs Smith." Tommy reminded him, though he was sad to break the happy mood, "I'll get a message to her, asking that she might arrive after dinner. Then you can get it over with."

"Yes." Hans became solemn again, "I hope she forgives me."

"For what?"

Hans pulled a face.

"I'm not really sure. I… I just feel that somehow I could have done more."

"Then I think you better begin by forgiving yourself."

Chapter Twenty

Seylon Hall had been built in 1614, a fabulous old building of red brick and twisting chimneys. In the eighteenth century, when the first great guides to the architecture of Brighton were being compiled, a local vicar had passed by Seylon Hall and declared it a masterpiece. He sketched the building and from this an engraving was produced and then reproduced in the Hathaway's Guide to Brighton and Hove. After that Seylon became the favourite view for the amateur artist and the family complained of the large numbers of people who appeared on their lawn every day in the summer months to draw or paint the house.

Time, however, had not been kind to the hall. As the Seylons' changing fortunes ebbed so too did repair work on the family abode. Leaks in the roof went unattended, damp on the walls was masked by paint and the whole place began to rot in on itself. With the dwindling of the family funds in the nineteenth century, the house showed the first outward signs of its neglect. The east wing suffered first, the roof caving in after a bad fire ate through the first floor. An elderly Swedish butler was blamed for the calamity which resulted in the necessary demolishing of part of the property, but local thinking was that it had been bound to happen eventually. The stables went next, blown down in a storm. They had stood empty for decades, fortunately. Then the west wing bedrooms became uninhabitable due, yet again, to the roof.

By then the grounds had become overgrown and unmanageable, though the family still employed a solitary gardener. The once fine lawn where budding artists had sat and sketched was now a heap of molehills and daisies. When Joshua Romulus inherited the hall from his father it was a ramshackle place. The west wing was virtually abandoned, the attics were in such a bad state the servants refused to go up into them, less they come crashing back through the floor. Instead they slept in the bedrooms at the east side of the main hall. Joshua confined himself to one large bedroom on the west side, nearest the creaking joists and groaning walls of the abandoned wing. On occasion, it was said, you could hear voices in the forgotten rooms.

Joshua did no more to the house than his parents or grandparents had. It limped along, just managing to survive long enough to provide a home for him in his old age. Then, so local legend had it, at just the moment Joshua went into the family vault the west wing collapsed down on itself in a flurry of plaster dust and splitting beams. It took most of Joshua's bedroom with it. After that everyone knew it was only a matter of time before the main hall fell. Haste was made to remove what valuables remained, largely the library, and what was left was scavenged for nearby homes.

On the night of the 12 November 1901, so the story went, there was a terrible storm and lightning struck the abandoned hall. Flame engulfed the Seylon home and the conflagration could be seen for miles. By the time the fire had died down the next morning there was nothing but a hollow shell left of the 'masterpiece of Hove'. Local builders salvaged anything they could, leaving the rest to nature.

Or at least that was the legend Clara told Dr Deáth as

they rode through an old set of gateposts, long shorn of their iron gates. She had compiled it from several local history books including the one by Joshua Romulus.

"Time is really rather cruel." Deáth reflected as his horse picked its feet over the remains of an old driveway.

An avenue of limes still stood as a reminder of a once formal and grand entranceway.

"Had the Seylons been sensible they would have sold the house and established themselves in something more affordable. Or gone into business." Deáth continued, gently nudging on the horse with a twitch of the reins.

"I somehow don't think that is how one does things when one is part of the nobility." Clara smiled.

"Well then, even more foolish!" Deáth laughed.

The avenue dissolved into a long view over what had once been open grass lawns and parkland. In the eighteenth century the scene would have been dazzling, with deer grazing and the manicured grass stretching out like a huge green carpet before the house. Today it looked rather more like boggy heathland and the horse stumbled a little as they dropped down a shallow slope.

"Is that it?" Deáth pointed to a small mound ahead, fragments of stone could just be seen poking through the grass.

"I imagine so." Clara said.

Deáth negotiated the horse across a patch of barely visible gravel and then they were trotting across what had once been a formal lawn. The lumps and bumps ahead slowly resolved themselves into the visible, rectangular outline of a building. They pulled up just in front of three long stones, stacked on top of each other, which must have formerly been the steps up to the door.

Clara jumped off the buggy seat and walked up the steps. She found herself standing on the last traces of a tiled floor. She scrubbed her heel on a stone.

"Poor Joshua Romulus. Look at your home!"

"Since we believe Mervin's stash is in the cellar, I suggest we make haste and find it before we get soaked."

As Dr Deáth spoke a raindrop splashed on Clara's face.

"I agree."

They split up and went in search of a cellar entrance. The layout of the old hall was still just visible and Clara theorised a cellar would be located at the back of the building near the kitchens. Stepping into a black and white tiled room she found what appeared to be a melted lump of iron; seemingly the last remains of a cooking range. A little further on there was a gap in the grass covered stones which suggested a doorway. Just beyond that was a mass of brambles and, very difficult to see in their midst, a stone staircase leading into the ground. It seemed to emerge from nowhere and Clara came close to stumbling straight into the cellar.

"Over here!"

Between then Deáth and Clara removed as much of the brambles as was possible and revealed a dark hole leading downwards. Deáth still had the lamp and shone it into the darkness, there was not much to see beyond a grey set of steps.

"Do you suppose they are safe?" Clara risked a foot on the top step, it didn't seem to crumble beneath her.

"I suggest we take it carefully." Deáth peered down the hole, "I see far too many deaths caused by falling down cellar steps."

"That's a comfort." Clara braced her foot on the next step, they were rather steep and it was best to place the foot sideways to get a grip. She reached out a hand and felt a wall.

"There was one case I recall, a big house like this. The cellar door was rather poorly placed next to the door for the dining room. One evening the lady of the house rushed down to dinner, the gas had yet to be lit, and in her haste she opened the wrong door. I hear that nowadays they keep the cellar door locked."

Clara was now treading into darkness, as Deáth held the lamp, and his stories were not particularly helping. Each footstep was somewhat a leap of faith as she could not see anything beyond the step she was on.

"That was an accident, but I do know of a servants' quarrel that resulted in one being pushed by the other down a set of cellar steps. Poor fellow broke his neck."

"I can imagine." Clara felt apprehensively with her hand along the wall.

"Then there was a case involving an old shop cellar, one of those ones which have an entrance up through the pavement covered by a trapdoor. Well this particular trapdoor had seen better days and this rather solid lady walked over them and it gave way beneath her. She survived, but there was a fellow stacking boxes in the cellar below whom she landed on and killed."

"Really?" Clara wished Deáth would shut-up. She put out her foot and felt solid ground. She paused for a moment, cautiously felt about further and relaxed. They had reached the bottom.

Deáth joined her and held up his lamp, it only cast a thin circle of light, but enough to just make out a brick wall on their right.

"I smell foxes." He said.

"Right," Clara took a pace forward, "We were facing the west wing when we descended, the east wing was behind us, so the far north corner should be this way."

She felt her hand along the wall to her right and as she expected it suddenly fell away revealing a further section of the cellar. They walked together into a large, black void. It was impossible to know its boundaries for the light would not stretch far enough. So they kept walking forward, watching out for stones or roots on the floor that might trip them, until the light showed them the far wall. They stopped.

"I suggest we try the right hand corner first." Deáth said.

"Why?"

"People favour the right side of places for some reason, if you do tests on a group asking them to randomly choose to go left or right, they most often go right."

"Really?" Clara turned her head right into pitch darkness.

"Or I may have just made that up." Deáth pondered, "I thought I read it somewhere?"

"Let's go right." Clara decided, not wanting to delay further.

The cellar was quite large, but was completely empty aside from the odd scuttling rat. There was a damaged rubber ball and a forgotten small cap lying on the floor that suggested children had visited the place to play in, or at least explore. Perhaps there had been other activities down here, but it was so dark and dank Clara could not imagine it a place many people would want to spend time in. They found the right corner and Deáth shone the light on the ground.

"We have to assume he buried whatever it was he kept his stash in." Clara went down on one knee and felt the soil, it seemed a little less compacted than the dirt around her, but after 15 years who knew what a floor might look like?

Deáth found a shard of wood propped against the wall and put it to use as a rudimentary shovel. He dug around in the soil for a while, making a large circle in the floor without coming across anything in particular. After about ten minutes he stopped.

"Let's try the other corner."

They headed to the other side of the cellar and at once Clara felt they were in the right place.

"Look!" Drawn on the wall was a black hand print, someone had taken a piece of charcoal and traced the outline of their hand onto the wall, repeating the process several times to darken the mark, "That has to be a sign left by Mervin. He wouldn't, after all, expect Penny to fudge around in the dark."

Deáth cast his light onto the floor, but yet again there were no obvious marks of disturbance. He picked up the shard of wood and with the lamp passed to Clara he attacked the floor in the spot just beneath the black hand mark. They were both surprised when almost at once the shard of wood hit something solid. Deáth got down on his knees and pried up loose soil with his fingers. A rectangular hole began to emerge and as Clara cast the light of the lamp on it something glittered, albeit dully.

"It's a box!"

It was, in fact, a security box, the sort used by shopkeepers or restaurant owners to store a day's takings before it could be transferred to a safe or bank. As Deáth started to pull on the box it became plain it was locked.

"There was a key with that note left for Penny." Clara pulled out the rusty key from her pocket and fitted it in the lock. The lid came open and the lamplight shone on bank notes and coins. They had found Mervin Grimes' ill-gotten gains.

"I'll take that." There was a click behind them. Clara swung the lamp and saw the ghoulishly outlined face of Gregory Patterson. He was holding a pistol.

"You followed us here." Clara said.

"Penny told me all about the stash and the ring, but even she wasn't quite sure where Mervin had hidden everything. She didn't make the connection between the vault and the ring."

"We have no interest in the money. You may take it." Dr Deáth said, his eyes on the pistol.

"No he may not!" Clara said sternly.

Before Deáth could counter her, she doused the light of the lamp and they were all plunged into darkness.

"No one move!" Patterson yelled.

"Do you even know how to use that gun?" Clara said from somewhere in the darkness.

Patterson, unable to see, pointed the gun at shadows. There was a crunching noise as someone moved, but he couldn't pinpoint the spot.

"I only want to retire from that damn shop!" He cried out to nobody.

"It's not your money Mr Patterson. For that matter it was never really Mervin's either."

A match flared by Patterson's ear and he saw Clara standing by his side out of the corner of his eye. He started to swing round the pistol. Clara reached out and grabbed his arm.

"Let's not be silly Mr Patterson. I have already concussed a gangster this week and I am holding a very heavy lamp at the perfect angle to bring it down on your skull, which would be most inconvenient for us both as I am sure the force will smash it."

Patterson's arm was trembling under Clara's fingers.

"You're not a killer Mr Patterson." Clara tightened her grip slightly on his wrist. His fingers twitched and then the gun fell to the floor, "Dr Deáth, would you mind holding his arms while I relight the lamp?"

Deáth moved behind Patterson and pinned his arms behind him, while Clara lit another match and rekindled the flame in the oil lamp. It was good to bring light back to the dark cellar. Clara picked up the pistol, then pulled the opened security box out of its hole.

"Is there room in your buggy for three?" She asked Deáth.

"Not really."

"Then we will have to be very cosy, because I'm not standing out in the rain waiting for you to return for me." Clara looked Patterson full in the face, "Is it really so bad running a bookshop?"

"Worse than you can imagine." Patterson said miserably, "Couldn't you just shoot me?"

"I solve murders Mr Patterson. I don't cause them." Clara nodded at Deáth and they turned Patterson around to head for the stairs.

"I only wanted to take a rest. Just a little one. Maybe a holiday in the sun, somewhere." Patterson was half sobbing to himself as he walked, "Why is life so unfair?"

"For that Mr Patterson," Clara said as she walked beside him holding up the lamp, "I suggest you ask Mervin Grimes."

Chapter Twenty One

"And this is my sister Clara." Tommy introduced Mrs Smith to Clara.

It was just gone 9 o'clock and the good lady had foregone her usual early bedtime to make allowances for the Fitzgeralds' late dining hour. She had arrived just after Annie had cleared the last plates away from the table and Tommy had ushered her into the parlour where Clara was sitting in an armchair with a cup of cocoa. She felt she had earned it after the day she had had.

"Please take a seat Mrs Smith, I must just attend to our other guest."

Mrs Smith sat in the armchair opposite Clara while Tommy departed to fetch Hans. She looked tired, perhaps exhausted would be the better word.

"Would you like tea or cocoa?" Clara offered.

"No thank you." Mrs Smith removed her gloves and folded them neatly on top of her handbag, "I appreciate the efforts you have gone to for me."

"Not I, Mrs Smith, Tommy has worked on this case alone. I'm afraid I was rather distracted with another matter."

"Well then, I appreciate his help."

Annie entered the room with a fresh pot of tea. She offered a cup to Mrs Smith, who again declined. She looked pinched around the face, as if the very act of swallowing tea would be painful for her.

Tommy returned, Hans Friger a pace behind him. Hans looked almost as worried as Mrs Smith. When they entered the room Mrs Smith started to stand, but Hans waved her back into her chair.

"Please Mrs Smith, not on my account."

Mrs Smith's face changed when she heard his German accent. A splash of colour came to her cheeks. Clara realised the desperate woman was trying to gather if this could possibly be her long-lost son, despite his appearance being almost completely different to Jurgen's. Clara thought it best to intervene swiftly.

"May I introduce our guest Mr Hans Friger?"

Hans gave a very Teutonic bow to the good lady. Something faded from Mrs Smith's face, a dullness crept over her. She rearranged her gloves on her handbag.

"Hans can explain what happened to your son." Tommy felt the situation was becoming more awkward by the moment.

"He is dead then?" Mrs Smith bit her lip, "I really should have known…"

"Madame, I have spent these last two years hoping to find you." Hans moved forward and crouched before Mrs Smith, "Your son was a very good man. That is the first thing I have wanted to tell you all this time. The second is that he passed away peacefully and was not in pain."

"What happened to him?"

"He was travelling home to you when he became sick with the influenza. There was nothing anyone could do."

Mrs Smith nodded her head, she seemed to have shrunk considerably.

"I had no address for you, so I could not return his things. But I kept them safe nonetheless." Hans picked up the parcel he had left on the parlour table that morning and set it in Mrs Smith's lap.

For a long moment she looked at it numbly. Tentatively she took the end of a piece of string between her fingers and pulled. The knot jerkily unravelled and slipped away, the brown paper sprung open a little. With trembling fingers she pushed back the folds of paper and revealed a handful of contents. On the top was a beautiful pocket watch, still ticking away the time in precise, little seconds. Next there was the photograph of herself and her husband and under that a pile of postcards and letters that she had sent to Jurgen over the course of his internment. Mrs Smith picked one out and read her own tight handwriting describing the mundane news that April 1917 had been rather cold and her daffodils were suffering under a blanket of frost. Tears welled in Mrs Smith's eyes. The words blurred and then she put one hand to her face and sobbed silently.

It seemed only polite for the men to leave. Clara remained with Mrs Smith, letting her cry and release her long-held sorrow. Annie stirred two lumps of sugar into a cup of tea and waited patiently to hand it to Mrs Smith when she recovered herself. It took several minutes before the flood could be stopped and Mrs Smith was finally able to look at them again. She accepted the cup of tea without hesitation this time.

"I wanted better news for you." Clara said, "I'm sorry."

"I only hoped a little that he was still alive." Mrs Smith took a long sip of tea, "This... this is good too. Because now I know."

Clara nodded.

"Is there anything else I can do to help?"

Mrs Smith gave a long sigh.

"I think not. " She finished her tea and stood to place it on the table, "You have been very kind, now I need to go on my way and think about what must come next."

"Take care Mrs Smith." Clara said, "Call on us if you need anything."

Tommy and Hans had retreated to the dining room and that was where Clara found them.

"Thank you Hans, though the news is sad Mrs Smith

at least now has answers." Clara said to the German at her table.

"That is all right, it was the least I could do for Jurgen." Hans was silent a while, "I miss him too, so many people don't care for Germans these days."

"The war muddled things." Tommy said softly.

"You were in it then?" Hans asked.

Tommy clenched and unclenched his hands.

"Yes."

"And your legs?"

"Let's just say I have as good a reason as any to hate Germans."

Hans placed a hand on Tommy's shoulder.

"Then your kindness towards myself and Mrs Smith is all the more gratefully accepted. I am sorry our countries had to go to war."

"Well, we are all still just people." Tommy said, a gruffness in his tone masking his embarrassment, after all he had considered turning Mrs Smith done simply because she was German, "Just the lingo that's different."

Hans smiled at him.

"Is that all?" He teased.

"Well, I am exhausted." Clara announced to them both, "So I am off to bed."

The boys said good night and Clara made her way upstairs. She hadn't been exaggerating about being exhausted, she felt positively shattered.

"I need a holiday." She groaned to herself, then smiled. For a holiday she would first need to start finding clients who paid!

Chapter Twenty Two

Clara slept late the next day and Hans had already caught the early train when she went downstairs. Tommy was complaining about the book shop being closed in the parlour and reminded Clara that she would need to explain to him how she had happened to have his favourite bookseller arrested. This detective lark could be really inconvenient some days.

There was a letter for her on the hall stand and Clara decided to retire to the conservatory to read it. The mellow august sun was streaming through the windows and warming the old wicker furniture. She settled into a chair that creaked under her weight and thought about her mother sitting in this same room, going over her latest charity project. It was always something like making jam for the workhouse inmates or collecting blankets for the Lost Animals Home. Clara wondered what she would make of her daughter's current project, not exactly jam-making, but she supposed it might count as a charity case.

Clara let the nostalgic memories drift to one side as she opened the letter. It was post-marked Cornwall and written on paper headed 'Ruskin's Antiquities'.

Dear Miss Fitzgerald,

Thank you for your enquiry. Yes, I do recall the mummy of the pharaoh Hepkaptut which I sold to Bowmen's Carnival around a year ago. He purchased it with several other items of questionable provenance, which I was selling for a minimal price. I purchased Hepkaptut in 1914 from a gentleman in your hometown of Brighton. I have the receipt before me as I write and can tell you his name was Mr Henry Dawkins and he at one time ran a private museum. I include his address below.

I had doubts about the mummy, but was prepared to take a chance for the amount Dawkins was asking. Unfortunately Hepkaptut proved unappealing to my regular customers and I was most relieved when Mr Bowmen took him off my hands. I do hope this answers all your questions and I thank you for your interest. If I can be of any further assistance please do not hesitate to contact me.

Yours Sincerely
Donovan Ruskin

Clara felt the last dregs of exhaustion leave her as a new purpose came into view. She went for her hat and gloves, said a hasty goodbye to Tommy and then disappeared out the door. She made her way to Old Steine, the row of prestigious houses where Mr Ruskin had listed the private museum as once existing. Clara tried to remember, as she walked, if she had ever heard of Dawkins and his collection, but she could not say she had. She was certain, with two parents fascinated by both science and history, had the museum been a public enterprise, they would have surely visited it at some point.

Old Steine took the word 'grand' very seriously and the houses that fanned out around a picturesque garden were the finest creations late Georgian Brighton could offer. Admittedly the residents these days were, on occasion, of the sort who house-shared and one or two of the farthest houses had been sub-divided. But the central properties were still the reserve of the best families, those who kept ten servants whether they needed them or not. Mr Dawkins, therefore, had to have money to live here.

Clara found his house almost directly opposite where a statue of King George (she forgot which one) had formerly stood. Like its neighbours it was grand with five floors, including a basement set beneath street level. Yet most of the windows were tightly shuttered and there was an atmosphere of reclusiveness about the property. Clara went up to the front door and rang the heavy bell. It was a long time before anyone came.

"Yes?" A middle-aged woman in a housecoat answered. She was holding a scrubbing brush in one hand.

"I apologise for interrupting but I was looking for Mr Henry Dawkins?

"Well this is Mr Dawkins' house, but he don't receive visitors." The woman explained. She had a pinched face and greying curls that were roughly pulled back into a bun.

Clara assumed she was the housekeeper.

"Might I present him with my card? It is really rather important I speak with him, it is about his museum."

"Mr Dawkins doesn't run a museum anymore, not since he became ill. Mr Dawkins is a very sick man."

"I'm very sorry to hear that."

"It's cancer. Doctors are amazed he is still with us at all." The housekeeper gave a choked sniff and hastily rubbed at her nose with the hand holding the scrubbing brush, "I've been here thirty years, seeing Mr Dawkins this way just tears me up. He don't see people at all these days, miss."

"Could you ask him to make an exception for me? It really is important. One of the artefacts that used to be in his museum has returned to Brighton and questions are being asked about its authenticity. I am trying to trace its provenance back beyond the time it was in Mr Dawkins' museum."

The housekeeper looked torn.

"I don't like people criticising Mr Dawkins."

"That is why I must speak to him, to clear up this matter before rumours spread around Brighton concerning the item."

"He is just so very sick."

"I will not disturb him for long, I promise." Clara aimed to look as sincere as she could.

The housekeeper hesitated.

"Mr Dawkins does like talking about the museum. It broke his heart having to sell it, but how could he keep it running when he has to rest in bed all day? I thought maybe he would keep a few bits, but he said it reminded him too much. Used to be all the front rooms were set up with displays of objects and he had typed information cards for everything. It was a treasure trove. Then he had to sell it and now we keep the rooms shut up. He can't bear seeing the rooms empty."

"That is very sad." Clara concurred, "I wish I had known of the museum while it was still open."

"I think you would have liked it miss. It was very informative." The housekeeper paused, then made up her mind, "I'll go see how Mr Dawkins is feeling, but I make no promises. If he isn't fit for visitors so be it."

"I understand."

"If I can ask you to wait in the hall miss. Excuse the smell, I try to keep things clean."

Clara stepped inside and was struck by a strong odour of disinfectant. Her mind flashed back to her days of nursing in the hospital and the endless battles waged by orderlies to try and keep the building clean. It seemed the housekeeper was on a similar, one-woman, mission.

She waited patiently, examining the doors of the shut rooms. They were each locked as if the precious treasures Dawkins had once hoarded still resided behind them. What it must be like to put your life into such work only for illness to snatch it from you. Sickness was a cruel thing. Clara concluded, far, far crueller than death itself.

The housekeeper clattered back down the stairs.

"He says he would like to talk to you, but I must warn you again miss that he is very ill and it might shock you a little."

"I worked in the hospital during the war, I am almost unshockable in that department." Clara assured her.

"Well then you will understand not to tire him too much?"

"Absolutely."

"And make sure he pauses and takes a drink regularly, else he will start to choke."

"I understand."

The housekeeper led Clara upstairs to the third floor along very empty, but also very clean, corridors, to a room set at the back of the house.

"I can't do anything about the smell." The housekeeper gave one last warning as she opened the door.

The room beyond was filled with sunlight, the brightness controlled by thin blinds at the windows which gave the light a strange hazy quality. Clara noticed the smell and recognised it as the last days of a dying man, the strange aromas of cleaning materials and a decaying body that only awaited the death of its owner to fully throw itself into decomposition. Mr Dawkins lay beneath several thick blankets and a quilt on the bed, a porcelain bowl propped on his right and a jug of water on his left. He was extremely pale and his skin clung to his bones like rubber, revealing every contour of his skull. He was probably not so old, perhaps in his early sixties, but he had the appearance of a corpse. He tilted his head slowly towards Clara and hoarsely welcomed her.

"Do come in!"

Clara approached the bed. Everywhere there were the tell-tale signs of a sick and dying man; the bottles of medicine, the syringes, the smells of chemicals, the untouched cups of tea and half-finished letters that had slipped from an exhausted hand onto the floor.

"Thank you for seeing me." Clara said, "I shan't disturb you for long."

"I don't mind if you do, dear. There is very little else for me to do."

"I'll let you talk." The housekeeper announced from the doorway, "I'll be back in half an hour precisely. Don't over-tire him."

She gave another concerned look at her employer and then vanished into the empty hallways of the house.

"Mrs Grebe cares a great deal." Dawkins said with a faint smile, "She has been in this house almost as long as me."

"If at any point you want me to leave…"

"Don't trouble yourself, dear lady. I shall make plain if such is the case, but I hope it will not need to be. Now, you want to talk about my museum?"

"Specifically about a former object from your collection whose provenance is being questioned. Namely…"

"Wait, don't tell me." Dawkins weakly held up a hand, he seemed adept at interrupting people, "Let me guess. Is it the stuffed Dodo? I always feared I had paid a great deal of money for an over-large pigeon?"

"Not the Dodo, no."

"Then it's the will of Oliver Cromwell that states he gives all his remaining wealth to Charles II?"

"Not that either, though I imagine that too is questionable."

"Yes, I fear so, but I came across it cheap in a bric-a-brac sale." Dawkins mused for a moment, "What about the Aztec Crystal skull supposedly engraved with the name of Cortez?"

"Perhaps I should just tell you as we only have a little time?"

Dawkins sighed.

"Very well."

"The object in question is the mummy of the pharaoh Hepkaptut."

"No!" Dawkins almost rose from his bed in surprise and alarm, "But he was one of my finest items!"

"Nevertheless," Clara said as gently as she could, "It has been questioned whether he is really Egyptian or, for that matter, ancient."

Dawkins sank back into his pillows, drawing the blanket up beneath his chin and clutching it with both hands.

"Hepkaptut." He whispered, "He used to stand in the green bedroom, second floor, third door on the right. I called that my Ancient Antiquities room. I had a fine collection of Egyptian Scarab beetle carvings and a Peruvian shawl that was at least 1,000 years old and found high up on a mountain. Hepkaptut stood in the centre, facing the door, so the first thing people saw when they entered was his face. I scared my dear old aunt by not warning her that he was there."

"Perhaps, you might recall how the mummy came into your possession?" Clara hinted.

"I really can't believe he was a fake. I know I was not perfect with all my finds, I mislabelled a child's black marble as a Roman jet bead once, but that was an honest mistake. I always tried my hardest and my museum gave great pleasure to those who visited. It was not a public thing, you know, people had to make an appointment, but I never turned anyone away. Children always loved looking at Hepkaptut as I told the story of his origins."

"But how did you come to have Hepkaptut?" Clara pushed, fearing Dawkins was a man whose train of thought ran in all directions at once and only occasionally collided with a relevant piece of information.

"Hmm?" Said the old man.

"Who did you buy Hepkaptut off?"

"Oh some lady. Now who is questioning his authenticity?"

Clara refrained from sighing in frustration.

"Mr Dawkins, the current owner of the mummy has some doubts. By tracing the provenance of the item and tracking down those who have come into contact with it recently, I hope to definitely prove one way or the other whether the mummy is real or not." It was a white lie, but Clara didn't see there any need to trouble a sick man with the news that he once had a murder victim on display in his house. There was no knowing how he would take such information.

Dawkins pursed his lips.

"Mrs Grebe can probably pull out the account book with the full details of the sale, but I remember most of it myself." Dawkins coughed a little, "It was 1912, or there abouts. I had spread the word that I was interested in unusual objects for my collection and I would get the occasional visitor knocking on the door with something to show me. One day this gentleman, well, that's rather generous, this man knocked on my door and told me he had been sent by a lady with an ancient mummy to sell and would I be interested? Naturally I asked a lot of questions and the answers seemed satisfactory, and I agreed to take a look at this mummy if it was brought to my house."

Dawkins began to cough harder. Without hesitation Clara reached out for the pitcher of water by his bed and poured out a glass. She held it to Dawkins' lips and he drank some gratefully. Refreshed he was able to continue.

"A day later this cart appeared with a large packing crate on top. I had it brought into the house and opened and there was Hepkaptut. The story I was told by the lady's agent, was that her uncle had gone abroad and spent time around Egypt. When he returned home he came with the usual souvenirs and one mummy. He had died that winter and the mummy was looking for a home."

"Do you recall the lady's name?"

"I dealt with things through her agent. His name was Mr William Brown..." Dawkins stopped because Clara had given an abrupt start, "Are you all right?"

"Billy Brown." Clara muttered to herself, then, "I apologise Mr Dawkins, the name rang a bell."

"In any case that is who I bought the mummy from."

Dawkins continued, "He was in this house almost two years, then I was diagnosed with this awful illness and it became plain that I was going to have a great deal of difficulty maintaining my museum. I decided to sell off my collection before I became too ill. As each room was emptied I had it locked up, so I need not see all my things gone. In my imagination, you know, I still picture those rooms as they were. It brings me some comfort."

"I'm glad to hear that." Clara said honestly.

There was little more to be said and Mrs Grebe arrived precisely after half an hour, as she had promised. Clara said her goodbyes and thank yous to Mr Dawkins and then followed the housekeeper downstairs. As she was putting on her hat Clara turned to the woman.

"Such a shame."

"I know." Mrs Grebe's face fell, "I think this winter will be the end of him."

"Thank you again, for letting me meet him."

"Well," Mrs Grebe said stiffly, "Maybe it cheered him up a bit."

Clara said a final goodbye, then headed out purposefully towards Brighton police station.

Chapter Twenty Three

"Well, well, here we are again." Inspector Park-Coombs said to Billy 'Razor' Brown who sat before him in handcuffs.

Clara had very briefly informed the inspector of her latest piece of information and insisted she speak to Brown. The inspector, dubious as always, allowed the interview on the condition that he be present at all times. Clara did not hesitate to agree, she would have suggested his presence had he not offered it.

"So this time its assault we are dealing with." Park-Coombs fluttered a piece of paper at Brown.

"She assaulted me! Nearly killed me!" Brown glowered at Clara indignantly.

"You appear to forget you were in my house." Clara said.

"Doctor says you could have cracked my skull!" Brown complained.

"You mean I didn't?" Clara gave him a perplexed look, "I really thought I hit you quite hard. You must have a thicker skull then I imagined."

Brown snarled at her.

"Could we do this without the bickering?" Park-Coombs raised an eyebrow at them both.

Clara quickly regained her composure.

"Tell me about the mummy you sold to Mr Dawkins' museum in 1912 Billy." She said.

Billy was caught off-guard.

"What?"

"You sold Hepkaptut, or rather Mervin Grimes, to Mr Dawkins in 1912. He kept a receipt from the sale."

Billy went into moody silence.

"I should add," Continued Clara, "That this proves you did not know about the significance of the ring back then, unlike how you explained things to me. You must have learned of the ring more recently, from Gregory Patterson, for instance?"

Billy glared at the table, saying nothing.

"Really Mr Brown," Sighed the inspector, "Silence is more unhelpful to you than us. Patterson has told us everything about his plan, he is very afraid about going to prison. Do you really intend to keep silent for people who don't give a damn about you?"

Brown had a grimace on his face. He was quiet for several moments, then a little voice inside him asked the same question the inspector had, why was he keeping mum? They already knew enough to put him in a lot of hot water, if he said nothing those who got him into this mess would go free. Brown slowly raised his head.

"All right, Patterson approached me. Knew me from the days when Penny was still alive. She had told him about the ring, but he didn't know everything. In any case, he had been at that fair wandering about the stalls, and suddenly there was this mummy wearing Mervin's ring. He didn't really give much thought into whether the mummy were real or not. Just got in touch with me and asked me to steal it."

"But you knew that the mummy was Mervin Grimes, yes?"

"Bit of a shock seeing it there. I got rid of the thing in 1912 and after that I gave it no thought. But there was Mervin in a glass case, screaming at everyone. Soon as I saw him I knew I would have to do more than just steal that ring."

"But the ring was the priority."

"Always. Patterson said we would split the stash." Brown's eyes flicked about the room, his mind was on the double-cross he had planned to do to Patterson. It didn't matter now, of course, "Yeah, seeing Mervin like that was unsettling."

"So who gave you Mervin to sell in the first place?" Park-Coombs interjected.

"Haven't you worked that one out?" Brown laughed at them, "It was his ma, weren't it? She came to me one day and said she had a job for me. She had a body to sell. To sell? I says. You don't sell bodies! But this one she reckoned she could because of the condition it was in. She had this plan to fool an old fella who ran a private museum. She showed me the body, didn't say it was Mervin, naturally, but I only had to see that big old ring to guess. Could even still see the mark where I tried to hack it off! Anyway, we tarted him up as some ancient pharaoh and I put on my best suit to fool this old codger in his museum. It worked too."

Clara slipped back in her chair. So all along it had been Mrs Grimes. No wonder she was so sure he was dead, she had killed him! Clara closed her eyes for a moment, running back through that first conversation with the woman. Had there been a clue there? All she could remember was the woman's apparently genuine grief.

"I think that's all we need from you today Brown." Park-Coombs nodded to the constable at the door, "Take him back to his cell, and if he escapes again heads will roll!"

Brown gave them a sneer as he was led away.

"Was that what you expected?" The inspector asked Clara as soon as he was gone.

"Not really."

"We have no real evidence except Brown's testimony, and I can tell you how much that would count in a court of law."

"You don't need to say it inspector, to catch Mervin Grimes' killer we would need a confession."

"And how do you propose we get that?"

"Ask?" Clara suggested.

The inspector laughed.

"So simple?"

"A mother who kills her child must feel something, one would hope. Perhaps a sympathetic ear would unleash her guilty secret?"

"So you'll go speak to her?"

"Worth a try?"

Park-Coombs thought over the matter.

"I'll send a police constable as back-up or to make the arrest should she confess."

"He must remain out of sight."

"Absolutely." Park-Coombs agreed, after a moment he grinned at her, "I wish I had seen you bash Billy Brown over the head with a poker."

"I'm rather glad you didn't. I suspect you would have enjoyed it too much."

Clara returned to the bleak terrace house where it had all begun. It seemed months rather than days ago she had stood on this doorstep wondering what reception she would receive from Mervin Grimes' mother, and all along, as she had discussed the discovery of his body, the woman had remained stony-faced, never revealing even a hint that she knew all too well what had become of her son. It was almost unbearable.

Clara rapped on the door, her heart beating faster than she had expected. She admitted she was a little afraid in a way she had never been before. Mrs Grimes had murdered her son, hidden and then sold his corpse. That takes a kind of coldness that has no qualms about killing a nosy stranger. When the door opened Clara almost expected a gun. Instead there was Mrs Grimes looking as small and worn as before.

"You again." She said dully.

"I have news about your son's case." Clara explained.

Mrs Grimes gave a slow shrug.

"Better come in then." She allowed Clara through the front door and started to shuffle down the hallway.

Clara found she had an irresistible urge not to move away from the door, her only exit.

"I don't imagine anything I say to you will be surprising." She said without moving.

Mrs Grimes turned and looked at her. There was neither sadness or guilt in her expression.

"I know Mrs Grimes, I know about it all. I've spoken with Billy Brown."

Mrs Grimes gave a sort of half-smile, at least the corner of her mouth twisted up and down.

"Is Billy well?"

"He is in the police cells, telling them all he knows."

"Oh?"

"Mrs Grimes, I know you killed your son."

Mrs Grimes shook her head.

"No, wasn't me."

"Then how did you come to have his body? You killed him, hid him somewhere and then, for God knows what reason, you decided to sell him!" Clara had lost her patience, the woman was despicable, that was the only word for it.

Mrs Grimes gave a long sigh but said nothing. Then Bob appeared from the back room. He stepped solemnly into the hallway and stared at Mervin's mother.

"Is it true?"

Mrs Grimes knitted her hands together before her and stared into nothingness.

"I tried to be a good mother." She mumbled.

"Is it true?" Bob demanded, his temper rising a fraction so Clara took a pace forward.

"Please Mrs Grimes, you might as well explain how it happened." She said.

"My Mervin was never grateful for what I had done for him." Mrs Grimes cocked up her chin, a proud look on her face, "I spent my life working my fingers to the bone for him, and what did I get in return? Nothing! Just trouble. Twenty years looking after that lad and when he came old enough to look after me, did he? Did he care? No! Just wanted to go out with that fancy girl of his. Never a penny for his mother, never a little something so I might treat myself to a new hat or pair of gloves. Ungrateful he was, ungrateful!"

Mrs Grimes' hands dropped to her sides in fisted balls. Clara watched her apprehensively, she was, after all, a murderer.

"What happened that night? Why did you shoot him?" She asked.

Bob was watching from the other end of the hall, his expression a mixture of bafflement and fury. Clara had her eye on him too.

"That night!" Mrs Grimes snorted, "Mervin comes home proud of hisself. The horses come good, ma, I'm loaded now, he says. Loaded, says I, so can I have a bit for a new hearth rug? He laughs. Always thinking of the money aren't you, ma? You could give me a bit, says I. And you would only fritter it away and be as poor as the day you were born, says he, no, I'll keep a hold of it. Come on, get your hat, we'll go for dinner.

"So we did. Off to some restaurant he says is posh. I weren't impressed, my potatoes were cold and my gravy too thin. I says as much and Mervin gets angry. I bring Penny here, he snaps, and she likes it. She would! I say, she hasn't got no taste. And Mervin loses it there and then, but he won't do anything in that fancy restaurant, but I know what's on his mind. He's hit me before you know, what sort of a way is that to treat your mother?"

"So you came home?" Clara asked.

"I left the table. I said I was sick of this fancy food, all air and nonsense. I wanted decent food and Mervin was furious 'cos I was making a scene. But I didn't care. I stormed out and walked home. How is that, a son letting his old mother walk home alone at night? I told you, ungrateful. He always was, not like Bob here. Bob is a decent lad, my Mervin didn't know what decent was and to think I raised him with my own two hands. I tried to bring the lad up right, but he was wild!"

There was a pause, Clara was tempted to fill the silence, but she could see something working behind Mrs Grimes' eyes, so she kept her mouth shut. Bob started to speak but she gave him a glance that signalled he should stay quiet. It was another moment then Mrs Grimes began again. Her voice was choked, but it was difficult to say whether that was through grief or rage.

"I come back to this house and I takes off my coat and sits in the back room. I pick up some socks I been darning, Mervin's socks, mind! I was always good to him and he knew it. He took advantage. It must have been an hour before he slammed open the door. He were drunk, took after his father in that regard. Mother! He shouts. I ignore him until he stumbles through the door of the back room. You embarrassed me! He snaps. I say nothing, I was furious. How could a son talk to his mother like that? Would have been a time I would have slapped him one, but he was too big for that. He staggers into the room. I'm sick of your games! He yells. Games? I say. You treat me like a fool! He snaps, you think of no one but yourself. Well that riles me and I jump up. Speak for yourself Mervin Grimes! You is nothing but a selfish, spoiled brat that I is ashamed to have called my own!

"Mervin grows more agitated, he is pacing now. You want me to hit you, don't you? He cries out, you always push me too far. I wags my finger at him. You know nothing my lad, nothing! I have given everything to you and look how you treat me! He paces faster. I could kill you some days! He snaps, pointing his thick finger at me. They might as well try me for murder as for the other stuff I've done. You wouldn't dare, you're a coward, I yell back. I'm not scared of you! You should be! Well, I'm not! Who would be afraid of a street urchin who talks big, but is nothing more than a low level thug without principles!

Penny's proud of me! Mervin screams. Penny is little more than a street walker! I yell back, and then he really loses it. He comes at me, pushes me hard. I stumble and turn over a side table. The drawer falls out as I hit the floor and there is this pistol just inside. Mervin is almost on me, fists clenched, I shout at him to stay back, but there is this fury in his eyes.

"So I grab up the gun. Stay back! Stay back! You aren't going to shoot me mother! I will! I WILL! I have my finger on the trigger and I pull it back. Such a simple thing. There's a bang. Mervin grabs at his chest. What have you done? He slips to his knees and there he is dying, shot by his own mother. He stares at me a while longer, then he slumps forward and gurgles on the carpet. I nudged him with my foot, but he was gone."

"Where did you hide the body?" Clara asked.

Mrs Grimes gave a shrug.

"I thought about it for a while. Must have sat there looking at his body for an hour or so. The light had completely faded anyway. Upstairs, in Mervin's room, there is a cupboard built into the gap between the fireplace and the side wall, and I thought maybe that's where I would put Mervin. So I dragged Mervin upstairs and squeezed him into the cupboard."

"Wherever did you get an idea like that?" Bob said, utterly aghast.

"My husband." Mrs Grimes shrugged, "He was building a similar cupboard in our bedroom upstairs when he…"

Mrs Grimes shook her head.

"It was self-defence!"

"Up until the point you hid the body, and what about selling Mervin's mummy? That was hardly a very motherly act." Clara snapped, losing her rag with the woman.

"You don't know how it is!" Mrs Grimes yelled, "I had no money and I used to go peek at Mervin from time to time and his body had gone all strange. There was an article in the paper about these Egyptian mummies and Mervin looked just the way they were described. I had to do something!"

"I can't believe this." Bob trembled, "All this time... all the help I have given you, and it was you who killed him all along!"

Clara slipped back to the front door and opened it. Outside she caught a glimpse of the constable the inspector had sent to accompany her. She gave him a nod and he came to the house.

"Mrs Grimes, this policeman is here to arrest you." Clara said.

"Why?" Mrs Grimes declared in genuine astonishment.

"You killed your son."

"It was an accident!" Mrs Grimes suddenly turned and made a dash for the kitchen, but Bob was in the way and caught her in his arms, "Let me go! Let me go!"

The constable moved forward and there was a struggle between him, Mrs Grimes and Bob as he tried to make the arrest. Mrs Grimes kicked out with her feet yelling at the top of her lungs "Murder! Murder!" Bob wrestled with her, torn between holding her tight and not hurting her. In the end the constable managed to calm her enough to put on the handcuffs. Mrs Grimes swore at him, at Clara, and above all at the late Mervin as she was led to the door.

"He was a damn awful son!" She shrieked at them, "Look what he has brought me to!"

It was quite a relief when she was finally out the door.

"What now?" Bob asked. His face had split into a picture of misery, as though his world had fallen apart around his ears.

Clara gave him a gentle pat on the shoulder, not really knowing what to say.

"I need to look upstairs." She said.

She headed up the narrow staircase and found Mervin's room at the back of the house. A small, simply made cupboard stood against the wall, a thin rim of dust on its round handles. It had been built directly onto the wall to make the most of the limited space in the room. Clara opened it and was not entirely surprised to feel it was warm, a result, no doubt, of the fire burning in the grate downstairs wafting hot air up the connecting flue to this room. It was a perfect spot for mummification.

"No wonder she wouldn't let me paint this room. If I had opened that cupboard..." Bob said softly as he came up behind her, "To think he was here all along."

"She got the idea from her husband." Clara was muttering to herself. She stared at the cupboard a moment longer, then marched across the hall to the room normally occupied by Mrs Grimes.

This room also contained a built-in cupboard, slightly bigger due to the larger dimensions of the room and squeezed once more against the fireplace. Clara, rather gingerly, pulled the narrow double doors open. No grim, ghoulish mummy fell out at her. She was relieved, but it destroyed a notion she had just had. Clara shut the doors and stood back from the cupboard.

"What was that all about?" Bob gave her a curious look, but Clara said nothing because something had caught her eye.

"You are a carpenter Bob, if you were building a cupboard into a narrow space would you waste any inch of the room you had?"

Bob found himself struggling with this sudden change in direction.

"No?" He answered uncertainly.

"Exactly. But I would say that this cupboard has lost a good foot from the inside to the outside. See this portion here? When I open the doors there should be a niche behind it, instead..." Clara opened the doors and reached tentatively inside, "Black velvet, there is a sheet of black velvet masking off a section of the cupboard. Very clever, because it is so dark in this room you don't notice it."

Clara found one edge of the velvet and gave it a good

tug. It was fastened by wood pins and ripped as she pulled. Pins popped across the cupboard and loose strands of black velvet coated Clara's hands like shorn bristles. Then the top pins groaned and the sheet fell away. Clara stared into a hole revealed behind the cloth. In the space where the cupboard joined with the wall of the fireplace a body lay.

"Hello Mr Grimes." She said to the corpse, "So you were here all the time too."

The body of what, Clara assumed, had once been Mr Grimes was semi-mummified, sitting against the wall, the head tilted outwards. There was a rather obvious crumpled section of bone in his almost fleshless skull, as though someone had clobbered him hard with a hammer. Sitting just by his feet was a small pot of grout or plaster, rock solid, and lying across his lap a messy palette knife. It seemed he was in the process of neatening up the fireplace brickwork when he met his end. Clearly he had been Mrs Grimes' first victim and she stowed him where he had fallen, thus, twenty years later, giving her the idea of where she might hide her son's corpse.

"What's in there?" Bob called.

"Oh nothing, just Mervin's dad." Clara responded, "Looks like he didn't leave his wife and son after all."

Chapter Twenty Four

The summer had come to its end. August was slipping into September and children were returning to school as the last of the harvest cleared the fields. Clara made her way to the seafront to watch the fair dismantle itself and move on. They still had several more weeks of entertainment ahead before the icy days of January and February made them all think of finding a safe field to roll the caravans into and hibernate until Spring arrived. Clara walked unnoticed through the entrance, watching out for Bowmen. She doubted he would be best pleased to see her. The Brighton Gazette had been the first to break the news to the public that a murder victim had been hanging around the funfair, masquerading as an Egyptian Pharaoh. It had caused quite a scandal and more than one Puritanical local had decried the fair as the source of all evil. The Gazette's letter page had been abuzz with correspondents either defending or berating the funfair. Clara doubted Bowmen had appreciated this publicity, though it had at least drawn new punters to the fair under the misapprehension that Mervin Grimes' body had been reinstalled in the House of Curios for viewing. Someone had spread the rumour that because the body had been deceased for more than ten years it was no longer legally necessary to bury it and Bowmen was going to carry his corpse all across the country to regale crowds with the story of its origins and discovery. Naturally that was absurd, but quite a few people believed they would see the real body of Mervin Grimes at the fair.

Clara could only hope that Bowmen would forgive her interference and not refuse to return the following year. According to Brighton council the fairground had given a welcome boost to trade in the town and attracted almost as many visitors as in the days before the war. Surely Bowmen had done equally as well? Clara decided he was best avoided if she saw him.

She found her way to Jane Porter's caravan, past the semi-dismantled carousel. The Gallopers removed from their positions and tilted on their sides, glowered at her with their wild eyes. Never more frightening looking a creature had children been encouraged to ride; Clara sometimes had to wonder at British sensibility.

Jane Porter was standing at the door of her caravan beating a small rug with a broom handle.

"Good morning Clara. Off we go again!" She waved her arms at the fairground in the process of being broken down, "I believe we have a spot at Morecombe next."

Jane gave the rug a good whack. Her chin was dark with a five o'clock shadow many a man would have been proud of.

"Things seem to be improving." Clara said, giving her own chin a rub.

"Oh thank you. The medicine man gave me a tonic for baldness, seems to have worked a treat." Jane gave the rug another whack and then considered it sufficiently battered, "Sand gets everywhere."

"I just thought I would see you all off. I take it you know the news about Mervin Grimes?"

"Oh yes, utterly fascinating!" Jane shook her head at the madness of it all, "What is it they say? Truth is stranger than fiction?"

"I hope it hasn't caused too much disruption."

"I hadn't noticed anything." Jane shrugged, "Bowmen

might be of a different opinion, but ignore him. What will become of the mother?"

"It looks like they are aiming to claim insanity."

"And she killed her husband too? Goodness!" Jane considered the strangeness of the world as she perched on her caravan step, "You think you have seen every sort of crazy in a place like this, then you learn of something completely new."

"I hope it doesn't put Mr Bowmen off coming back to Brighton."

"Derek?" Jane laughed, "The profits he has seen here, you could hold a gun to his head and he would still come back!"

By late afternoon the fair was all gone, just odd patches of dead grass illustrating where it had been. Steam engines and horses were hitched to their loads and the caravans, rides and sideshows began another journey to their next stop. The seafront looked alarmingly barren with everyone gone. Clara felt a little shudder run down her spine, the year was turning.

Yesterday she had attended a funeral as one of only two mourners. The deceased had been Mervin Grimes, aka Dog-face Harry, aka King Hepkaptut, finally laid to rest in a pauper's grave. There had been no money for anything else; his mother did not have a penny to her name and the cash found in the hidden security box was from ill-gotten gains and could not be used for Grimes' benefit. Though exactly what was going to become of it was another dilemma. Inspector Park-Coombs was suggesting it go to the orphans' fund.

Bob Waters had stood beside Clara staring at the open grave, loyal to the bitter end. He looked like a kicked dog, his whole world turned upside down. Clara offered to buy him a cup of tea, but he had declined. He had a lot of thinking to do, or so he said. He stayed long enough to watch the unfortunate Mr Grimes snr end up in his own earthly abode; it was thirty years late, but better than being propped in a cupboard. It still boggled Clara's mind how Mrs Grimes had been able to sleep at night with her husband hidden in one cupboard and her son hidden in another. Perhaps she really was insane – or cold-blooded.

As for the murdering mother, her hearing was due in the autumn quarter and everyone was expecting her to be sent to London for her trial, the case being too scandalous and strange to remain local. Besides, popular opinion in Brighton was very against her. Mrs Grimes apparently still failed to see she had done anything wrong and denied all knowledge of her husband being buried in a wall. He had died from a heavy blow to the head, according to Dr Death, probably inflicted by a hammer. Mrs Grimes' neighbours were very disturbed to know they had been living next to rotting corpses all these years.

Then there was Billy Brown and Gregory Patterson. Brown was facing a long prison sentence for a string of crimes, everything from his activities with the Black Hand and onwards. The authorities seemed rather delighted to have him in their grasp. After so long thinking he was dead and safe from justice, they were rather rejoicing. Brown's trial was likely to be filling the newspapers all over Christmas, at least he was finally safe behind bars. It was still unknown how Brown had escaped from the Brighton police station to attack Clara and that troubled her. Park-Coombs wasn't saying much on the matter, but Clara sensed something was wrong, she just hoped it wasn't what she feared it to be.

Clara had heard less about Gregory Patterson, largely she suspected as he was rather dull in comparison to Mrs Grimes and Billy Brown. Aside from trying to steal a ring off a corpse and threatening the local coroner with a gun, his crimes were rather mediocre. The old bookseller was likely to get off with a lenient sentence taking into consideration his age and health. Still, it was unlikely he would ever be able to run a shop in Brighton again. He would find himself retired after all, just not in the manner he had anticipated. Clara found herself feeling a tad sorry for him, but only a tad, he had waved a gun at her after all.

"Hello Miss Fitzgerald."

Clara spun around from where she stood by the sea wall watching the fair roll away and found herself facing Mrs Smith.

"Hello Mrs Smith, are you well?"

"As can be expected." Mrs Smith gave a half-hearted smile, "I'm glad I spotted you, I want to give this to Tommy. To express my gratitude."

She unclipped her handbag and delved inside. Shortly her hand returned with a silver pocket watch, delicately engraved with flying birds.

"Mrs Smith…"

"Please don't refuse it." Mrs Smith pressed the watch into Clara's hands, "I want it to go to a good home. My husband engraved the birds upon it to symbolise hope and freedom."

Clara looked at the watch. It was truly a masterpiece of the watchmaker's art; the birds intertwined around each other and seemed alive with flight.

"I shall give it to him."

"Thank you." Mrs Smith managed that odd smile again, "I should get going, I am trying to put my life together at last and I have volunteered at the local library. I help stack and sort the returned books. It is a pleasing task and I don't have to speak to anyone."

"I really wish the best for you, Mrs Smith." Clara reached out and squeezed the woman's arm, "You always know where I am if you need anything."

"I'll remember that, good day." Mrs Smith walked away, a forlorn figure on the promenade.

Clara felt as though her breath had caught. The world seemed suddenly so dull and awful. She looked at the watch in her hands again, at the tiny birds cavorting on the silver. Each one a symbol of hope. She carefully clasped her fingers around the watch, so tight she could feel the faint tick of the mechanism. It was time summer came to an end; it had outstayed its welcome. It was time for a new season and a new case. Maybe this one would have a happier ending. Clara slipped the watch into her pocket and set off for home. Life, she decided, had a strange way of organising itself.

CPSIA information can be obtained at www.ICGtesting.com
Printed in the USA
LVOW11s2349100616

492108LV00001BA/30/P